DANGEROUS INTERLUDE

She turned slowly, hesitantly, and I took her in my arms again. I kissed the tears away from her closed eyes, and then she lowered her head and pressed her face against my chest. She lay very small and cold and still, and I knew she was still crying. I continued to caress her. I believed then that she was crying because it had been too soon, and because she feared that I would take it too lightly.

We still lay together when the explosion hit the *Shantung* like an almighty blow above the heart. The blast was deafening and the old freighter rocked and shuddered from stem to stern. It sounded and felt as though we had been torpedoed, except that a torpedo would have struck below the waterline and this impact had been too high and too close.

I catapulted out of the bed like a stung jackrabbit, snapped on the light and lunged for the door. I remembered that I was stark naked and paused to grab for my pants, and then I froze in a new numb shock of amazement.

Lin Chi was sitting up on the bed and with her left hand she held a sheet up to her small breasts. The tear stains were still on her anguished face, and in her hand there was a small black automatic that was aimed at my heart.

"Please, Johnny," she begged. "Please remain still. Do not make me have to kill you."

SEA
VENGEANCE
ROBERT CHARLES

PINNACLE BOOKS   NEW YORK CITY

SEA VENGEANCE

Copyright © 1974 by Robert Charles

A Pinnacle Books edition, published by special arrangement with Anglo-German Literary Agency

ISBN: 0-523-00946-1

First printing, November 1976

Cover illustration by Phil Marini

Printed in the United States of America

PINNACLE BOOKS, INC.
275 Madison Avenue
New York, N. Y. 10016

Sea
Vengeance

CHAPTER ONE

My nerves were on edge like pieces of raw catgut strung on a rusty fiddle and dreading to be scraped. The air was humid and the sun was a vicious white knife cutting beneath the hard peak of my cap and across my eyes. An hour ago I had put on a clean white shirt but now it was just a sweat-soaked rag, and even the stiff epaulettes with the three gold bars on my shoulders had gone soggy. The pain in my head bubbled and simmered just below boiling point.

In the port of Saigon the sun was always vicious, and at this time of year the air was always humid. It was a port where non-Asians stewed in their own sweat. At any time of the year my nerves would be on edge because Saigon was currently the most dangerous port in the world. I was never easy until the *Shantung* had sailed again to reach the sweet, salt air of the open sea, without being blown up by the Viet Cong.

I was thirty-eight years and one day old, and last night I had celebrated, and this morning the noise involved in loading the forward cargo hatch was enough to drive a sick man crazy. Already I had built up a hate complex towards the grinning Vietnamese who was operating the five-ton electric winch. The winch drum rattled and the cable screamed as he hoisted the last of the cargo nets aboard, and he seemed to take a fiendish delight in drowning out the constant clamour of shouting voices and roaring truck engines that made up the cacophony of sound that echoed aboard ship and along the wharf. The winch driver wore a wide coolie hat and a vest and baggy shorts like most of his dockside com-

1

panions, and so far I had bawled him out twice for his clumsiness.

I turned away to the rail and closed my eyes for a moment. My throat felt too hoarse for any more shouting. It was a mistake for a second later I heard Ching yell:

"Mister Steele, watch out!"

I turned on my left heel, shot my eyes open and looked up. The sun dazzled me but then a shadow swung over my face; the shadow of the cargo net careering out of control as the cable screeched off the winch drum. As it passed over my head I saw that one of the main ropes of the net was frayed and that the half inch strands of woven hemp were tearing apart.

I thrust myself hard away from the rail, hit the deck solid with my shoulder and made an undignified roll that brought me up tight against the low wall of the open cargo hatch. The rope snapped clean and one corner of the wildly swaying net dropped down to shoot out half its cargo of wooden boxes. Two of them went straight over the side, one crate hit the deck by my feet, and another broke itself asunder over the railing where I had just been standing and showered me with a cannonade of green apples.

Ching ran to help me up. James Ching was the *Shantung*'s Third Officer, a young Hong Kong born Chinese who divided most of his waking hours between work and study, and somehow managed to remain indefatigably cheerful about life. This was one of his rare moments without a smile.

"Are you hurt, sir?"

"No," I lied irritably.

I turned away from him but before I could vent my anger in the right direction there was a trumpet call from the bridge.

"Mister Mate!"

"Sir!"

I twisted my head up to see the bloated red face of Captain Leonard K. Butcher glaring down at me.

"What the hell's going on down there? Are you trying to sink my ship?"

2

"No, sir. I'm trying to keep the damned thing afloat!"

"Then for God's sake do it quietly. I have a head-ache."

The red face turned away and left me fuming and muttering fiercely under my breath. My own head throbbed abominably and the last thing I needed was to be told that *he* had a headache! At the best of times I found it difficult to love and respect my Captain, Sloppy Butcher who ran a sloppy ship, and in this moment I loved him least of all.

Ching had leaned over the rail and looked down at the dockside where a jabber of excited voices reached up to our ears.

"No one is hurt, sir," he reported. "But one of the crates is in the water."

I didn't care. I was already heading for that ham-fisted apology for a winch driver. He had locked the gears and gave me an apologetic shrug of his scrawny shoulders without bothering to remove that cursed grin from his face.

I called him a cross-eyed monkey and told him to get out of his seat and get the hell off my ship.

He knew that I was mad but he continued to grin and looked round for someone to translate.

I didn't speak Vietnamese, but we had a Chinese crew and I had managed to learn the best of their rude words during my fifteen years in the South China Seas. I let them fly and he looked startled, but still he sat tight in his seat.

I like to keep my temper, and I like to pride myself that I am a reasonable man—but everybody has an off-day once in a while. I was feeling ill, my shoulder was bruised and my head was pounding. This idiot had been making a muck-up of his job all morning, and I doubted that he had ever handled a winch before in his life. And that grin infuriated me. I clamped one hand on the shoulder of his grubby vest and hauled him bodily out of his seat.

He came away from the winch yelping protests in English.

3

"No, sir! No, sir! I am winch driver! This is my job!"

"Not any more it isn't! Not on this ship!"

I had exhausted my repertoire of the Chinese language anyway, and now that I knew he spoke English I cursed him some more in a way that we could both understand. I twisted him round and would have booted him off the ship, except that I suddenly found that I had an audience.

She wasn't beautiful but she was stunning to look at. She had a nice figure and she knew how to dress well and make the most of what she had. She wore tight white slacks with a broad, black leather belt with a decorated buckle, a bright red blouse and a Paris salon hat that was a white extravaganza with a wide, downward curving brim. That hat might have been too much, except that in this strong sunlight it shaded her eyes and became a practical choice. She looked cool and disdainful as she gazed at me across the cluttered deck.

"How very brave," she said. "Why, he's almost half your size!"

I looked down at the little man I was holding and realized that she was right. It did look bad. I was five foot ten inches of solid, well-fed Englishman, and yet I was physically assaulting five foot two inches of skinny, undernourished Vietnamese.

I let him go almost gently.

It seemed that everybody was staring at me, Ching, the girl, the Vietnamese shore party and the odd members of our own Chinese crew who had stopped to observe. The man who seemed to be in charge of the shore party was an older Vietnamese who wore faded blue overalls with a large number of tears and patches.

"Take this man off the winch," I told him. "And give the job to somebody who knows what he's doing."

I left them without waiting to see whether I had been understood and walked over to the girl. Under the large white hat her face was still cool, although a smile would have made her attractive, and I noticed a light dusting of freckles around her nose. Her eyes were a light honey brown to match.

4

I knew it was no good explaining that the little Vietnamese had damn nigh killed me with his clumsiness, and it would be even worse to add that I had the prehistoric grandaddy of all headaches. I had made a bad first impression and that was that. It was better to leave it there than to make excuses.

"I'm John Steele," I said slowly. "I'm Chief Officer of the *Shantung*."

"And I'm Evelyn Ryan."

I knew. I had read the passenger list and her name was at the head of it. Miss Evelyn Ryan, American nationality, aged twenty-eight, booked from Saigon to Singapore first class. The eight passenger cabins aboard the *Shantung* were all one class anyway.

Before I could welcome her aboard she remarked:

"You have a very learned vocabulary, Mister Steele."

I apologized. "I'm sorry about that little scene. It won't happen again."

Her eyes remained cool.

"It's unusual to find a man who can swear in Chinese."

I knew that we would never be friends and so I introduced James Ching. The Third Officer led her away to her cabin with a handsome smile and just the right mixture of courtesy and efficiency. She didn't bother to look back.

We resumed loading cargo with a replacement winch driver, and during the next hour I observed the rest of our mixed bag of passengers coming aboard.

A battered Renault taxi drew up to deposit an American couple in their late fifties. The man was heavily built, wearing grey trousers and a white shirt and suffering a necktie. His grey hair was still thick but receding gradually at the temples above a round, placid face, and he wore plain-rimmed spectacles. His wife was the homely sort wearing a powder blue cotton dress and a dark blue hat to shade her face. The passenger list had them noted as Catholic missionaries, Howard and Janet Deakin.

The next group of passengers emerged from a small

mini-bus. Eight Buddhist monks got out one by one and stood blinking uncertainly in the sunlight. With their close-shaven heads and bright yellow robes they made a vivid splash of colour on the dockside. They were seven young men, and one senior monk who led them slowly and sedately up the gangway in a calm yellow procession. I knew that they were a delegation bound for some obscure conference in Singapore.

The last of our passengers to arrive was a slender young Vietnamese woman wearing their delightful national costume, a high-collared tunic of pale bronze material, with long sleeves and slit at the hips over white silk trousers. Her face was a classic of delicate Asian beauty, and her long black hair was drawn back smoothly and tied into a long pony tail at the nape of her neck. Hong, our Chinese steward, led her past me as he escorted her to her cabin, and for a second I looked into her eyes. They were a lovely liquid black; eyes that a man could stare into for ever, but eyes which would never be so improper as to stare back. She smiled, and lowered her gaze demurely as she passed. She was listed as Miss Tho Lin Chi, aged twenty-five, also destined for Singapore.

Singapore was our next port of call, and I reflected that no one ever travelled on the *Shantung* any farther than they found necessary.

When the loading operation was completed I climbed up to the bridge to report. The wheelhouse was empty and Butcher was in his cabin, sitting behind a low table with his thick knees spread wide apart. He was a fat, untidy man in his sixties with a red, fleshy face. He had been bald as long as I had known him, and was rarely seen without his regulation cap with its peak full of gold braid. He was in his shirt-sleeves and he was sweating, and he needed a shave. He took as little pride in his own appearance as he did in his ship.

All the shore types who came to drink his gin and flaunt their importance had gone, and he was alone except for Jean Pierre Lassalle, our Chief Engineer. Between them the chess men had been set up. It was a very old set, the pieces carved out of smooth yellowed ivory into mandarins and warlords and Chinese foot soldiers and bowmen. The Captain spent most of his time in playing chess and drinking with Jean Pierre. The two of them were old friends who had been with the *Shantung* for too many years.

"The ship is cleared for sea, sir," I reported. "The hatches battened and all passengers aboard."

"And have you met the two ladies?"

Jean Pierre asked the question with a rakish slant to his eyebrow and a twinkle in his jaundiced eye. Except that they were of the same age he was a complete contrast to the Captain, a small dapper Frenchman he had spent a lifetime trying to imitate Maurice Chevalier. He even favoured a flat-topped straw hat when he pattered down the gangway for a night ashore. A few years ago he had carried the impersonation off well, but he had failed to mature with the real Chevalier, and now I found him pathetic. It was time he said goodbye to his departed youth and his straw hat.

Neither Jean Pierre nor the Captain had ever married, and I could not imagine that any woman would have wanted either of them. They had spent their entire adult lives in the China Seas. Jean Pierre loved his engines, although he pretended to be a rare ex-devil with the ladies, while if Butcher loved anything at all it was only the gin bottle.

"I have seen them," I admitted. "They're both good-looking, and I wouldn't be surprised if the Vietnamese girl speaks fluent French. That should please you."

"Ah, then I must brush up on my table conversation for tonight."

Butcher grinned. "You've been pickled in engine oil for too long, Old Frog. The smell will drive her away."

"Ah, no, my Fat Friend—if a girl is intelligent enough to speak French, then she will be sufficiently discerning to succumb to my charm."

I stood over them with my cap under my arm and reflected that at times they were like two senile schoolboys. Although no one but the Captain dared to call the Chief Engineer Old Frog, and no one but Jean Pierre dared to address the ship's master and stand-in for God as his Fat Friend.

Butcher looked up and asked me more formally:

"What was that racket about earlier this morning?"

"A cargo net snapped. They gave us a winch operator who couldn't ride a bicycle."

Butcher shrugged and pushed the gin bottle towards me.

"It's always the same. These damn shore-boys just don't know how to treat a ship. That's why I gave up trying to keep the *Shantung* clean. We're in port too often. Have a drink."

I shook my head. Sometimes when I looked at Butcher I was scared by what I saw, for I could occasionally see a frightening glimpse of myself in ten or fifteen years time. Already I was drinking too much, although last night had been a celebration and unusually excessive, and on this ship, in this heat, and in these seas, I couldn't see any real incentive to stop. As I saw it my only future was to skipper the *Shantung* when Sloppy Butcher finally drank himself to death, and the object lesson given by Butcher was that even a drunk could skipper the *Shantung*.

"No thanks," I said. "Not this morning."

"Suit yourself." Butcher was only slightly offended.

He rubbed his flabby jowl as he considered his next move, and I replaced my cap and quietly left them to their chessboard. I had two hours of the morning left in which to shower and sleep, and try to get some of the ache out of my head and the sludge out of my system, before the *Shantung* sailed for the open sea.

CHAPTER TWO

THE *Shantung* sailed an hour after noon with Butcher in command of the bridge. He was in a good mood, which meant that he had defeated Jean Pierre at chess, and showed no ill effects from his morning's intake of gin.

I was standing on the port wing of the bridge, with no duty to perform, but thankful to be saying farewell to Saigon. I had pity for the people of this unhappy land, but no love for their capital city. Once it had been the Pearl of the Orient, but that was too many years ago for me to care to remember. Now it was just a dirty city of corruption without a soul, soiled by the ravages of war, and with its prices inflated sky-high by the American occupation. Last night had cost me the best part of a week's pay.

Two ancient tugs manoeuvred us into the centre of the river, away from the cluttered mass of shipping and their attendant barges and sampans, and then reined back while their crews waved us on to the start of our forty-mile journey to the open sea. Those forty winding miles of the Saigon River carried more hazard than a typhoon on the open ocean. Mortar shells could bombard a passing ship from either bank, or a mine could be left drifting in the channel. The Viet Cong could turn a passage down this waterway into a lively trip.

In the bows Ching was leaning casually against the rail, a smart, slender figure beside the heavier bulk of Ho Wan, our Bo'sun. Wan was the biggest Chinese I had yet clapped eyes on, and sported drooping moustaches and a long black pigtail that made him look like a mandarin pirate. He claimed to have been born fifty years ago in a sinking junk in a storm, and the story he told in the crew's mess deck was that he had immediately left his mother's bed to sail the battered vessel into harbour. He was as much a part of the *Shantung*'s deck as the winches and the bollards, or the rust in the scuppers.

At the moment both Ching and Wan appeared to be standing idle, but I was not deceived. I knew that they would both be scanning the waterline for anything that might explode on impact, and that Wan would stay in the bows until we reached the open sea. The Bo'sun was the only man on board with sharper eyes than my own, so on that account I could relax.

I turned my head to watch Saigon receding, with the two tall red towers of the Baslica prominent on the skyline. As I did so Ralph Yorke came up the companionway from the boatdeck.

Ralph was the *Shantung*'s Second Officer, a fair-haired man in his early thirties. He came from Hampshire and brought with him a good nature and a ready grin. He also had a steady Eurasian girl friend in Singapore who no doubt helped to keep him good-natured and smiling.

"Good morning, Captain."

"It's afternoon," Butcher informed him.

Ralph shrugged behind his back and looked at me.

"Good afternoon, Mister Steele."

"Good afternoon, Mister Yorke."

Butcher always insisted that we were formal on the bridge. It was practically the only discipline he maintained.

By mutual consent we moved out to the far wing of the bridge and Ralph asked *sotto voce:*

How is J.B. this afternoon?"

"Steady on affable," I answered. "Like the rest of us he's glad to clear port."

As I spoke I reflected on the difference in our viewpoints. Ralph usually saw our Captain as Jolly Butcher, while to me he was always Sloppy Butcher.

We leaned on the rail for a while, watching the river traffic. Last night we had made a rowdy pair as we wheeled around the Saigon bars, and now we were content to be silent and let the freshening breeze clear away the last of our hangovers. There was a comforting sensation of movement in the ship, and deep down the engines thudded like a slow-beating heart.

Five minutes passed and then Ralph nudged my arm. "Am I dreaming, or is that for real!"

I turned round and saw that Evelyn Ryan had come out on to the boatdeck behind us. She still wore those white stretch slacks and the red blouse, although she had forsaken the Paris hat and now favoured a pair of dark glasses to shield her eyes. She had medium length chestnut hair, neatly waved and simply styled.

"She is for real," I admitted wryly, and explained to him how we had already met.

He had the nerve to grin at me. "In that case excuse me, Mister Steele. I think that at least one of the *Shantung*'s officers should prove himself a gentleman, and offer her the golden key to our happy ship."

"Watch out," I warned him. "She probably bites."

"Good. I like the kinky ones."

He turned away and I watched him descend briskly to the boatdeck, straightening the peak of his cap and squaring his shoulders with the two gold bars before he strolled towards her.

She turned as he approached. I didn't hear his opening line but I could see that it won him an instant smile. Soon Ralph had his shoulder propped against the lifeboat and they were chatting away like old friends. I had to admit that Ralph Yorke did have an enviable way with women.

I turned again to squint my eyes against the blistering sun, and watched our bows cleaving slowly through the dull brown waves of the Saigon River.

An hour dragged by. With the Captain on the bridge there was no need for me to be there but I stayed. Until we cleared Vietnam I liked to know what was happening. I used my binoculars frequently to scan the river banks and probe beneath the limp, heat-battered palm trees.

I saw buffalo plodding slowly in the rice fields, and

11

ramshackle fishing villages that were just a jumble of chicken huts built on stilts. At intervals an old man sat in a sampan, almost hidden beneath a big coolie hat, drowsing in the sun and invariably trailing a hand line into the water. I could almost swear that it was the same old man each time, a Viet Cong spy who appeared by magic around every new bend of the river.

Out here nobody was supposed to be Viet Cong, but everybody could be Viet Cong. I wouldn't have trusted the buffalo.

A junk veered past our bows, dragging its fat, heavy rump beneath a square, bamboo-stiffened sail like a lame kite. I gazed after it and the Deakins walked into view. Howard Deakin glanced up to see me standing on the wing of the bridge, and then steered his wife to the foot of the companionway.

"Hello, Captain," he called out. "May we come up and join you?"

I hesitated and looked through the open door of the wheelhouse.

"Captain Butcher, our passengers request permission to come up on to the bridge."

Butcher scowled. He didn't like passengers on his bridge, but when they asked politely it would be impolite to refuse them, and that was something that the company didn't like. He nodded reluctantly.

"Please do," I shouted down.

Deakin motioned to his wife to precede him and I gave her my hand as she stepped on to the bridge. Close up Janet Deakin looked worn and tired, and some of the strands of grey hair that escaped beneath her blue hat were beginning to turn white. She was thin and there were deep wrinkles around her eyes. Something had aged her, as though she had suffered a heavy loss, but she gave me a smile.

"I'm Howard Deakin." The missionary had a firmer grip, but there was something sad in his smile also.

I introduced myself, and tactfully added that Captain Butcher was in command of the ship. Butcher acknowledged them with a word and a nod, but then moved

12

over to study the binnacle as though at this unlikely stage it needed his undivided attention.

"You have a nice view from up here," Deakin said.

"The best on board," I conceded. And then in an effort to make him feel welcome. "Do you travel often by sea?"

"No, this is our first time on a ship. That's why I thought it would be nice to take a little sea voyage down to Singapore, before we fly home to the States. It's not a long voyage, so we're not likely to meet any big storms. I don't think that Janet and I would make very good sailors if the ship started to roll. We're what you would call born land lubbers."

"It's a smooth forecast all the way," I assured him. "Do you plan to stay long in Singapore?"

"Only a few weeks. We have some friends there, another missionary couple like ourselves. They run a small Catholic mission school and hospital, and they've offered us their hospitality for a while. Their name is Manson, perhaps you know them?"

I shook my head.

"The Mansons are from Pennsylvania." He seemed disappointed that I didn't know them. "We're from Ohio originally."

He reminisced about Ohio for the next few minutes, although I got the impression that it was a long time since either of them had seen their home state. Howard had pale, blue-grey eyes beneath his spectacles, and his round face was faintly yellowish, as though perhaps he had suffered from malaria and had been in Aisia for too long. His wife listened quietly, adding little to the conversation, but gradually I began to warm to them both. They seemed like nice genuine people.

An American jet went over our heads, high up in the sky and leaving a thin trail of white vapour like a pencil line across the blue. I identified it as a Voodoo, streaking on a reconnaissance flight, packed with electronics and cameras.

We gazed upwards, and out of the corner of my eye I saw Janet Deakin bite the corner of her lip and tremble.

13

Howard rested his hands on her arms and from behind and held her tightly.

I watched the Voodoo cross the sky and disappear, and then took careful stock of the bank and the palms, and the bend of the river ahead. All was peaceful and finally I looked back to our guests. The plane had disturbed them and I tried to put them at their ease.

"How long were you in Vietnam?"

"Fifteen years," Janet Deakin answered. There was bitterness in her voice and her faded blue eyes stared vacantly at the horizon.

Howard looked troubled, as though he felt that he should give me an explanation.

"We had a mission of our own," he said softly. "Nothing much, just a thatch-roofed schoolhouse and chapel, and a little clinic where we tried to help the sick. We are not doctors, we just had a little training in nursing before our Mission Society sent us out."

"It was in the Central Highlands." His wife took over when he stopped speaking. "It was very beautiful there—green jungle and green rice fields, and we had our own vegetable gardens. The war spoiled it all, but we were needed then even more. We had some good mission boys to help us."

They both fell silent, but they had been speaking in the past tense and I asked because I knew that they wanted me to know.

"What happened to it?"

Howard looked at me and said in the same quiet tone:

"Our mission was close to one of the American bases. Our helicopter gunships used to patrol the area regularly looking for Viet Cong. For a long time we believed that they could protect us."

"But one dark night the Viet Cong came?" I tried to help him out.

"Not exactly. It was just one Viet Cong. He climbed on to the roof of the mission after dark, then waited for the helicopter to pass on its patrol. Then he opened fire on the helicopter with a combat rifle. It was suicide of

14

course. The helicopter returned the fire full blast with its machine guns, and the Skyraiders were there within five minutes."

His eyes were blurred behind his spectacles.

"Janet and I were lucky to get out with our lives. We fled into the jungle to watch. The wing rockets from the planes demolished the buildings and within seconds there was nothing but a series of burning fires in the night. Half of our mission boys were maimed or killed."

"It was our life's work," Janet Deakin said. "All gone."

"I'm sorry." It sounded inadequate, but I didn't know what else to say.

Howard Deakin was silent for a long minute, but at last he said:

"If the Viet Cong had attacked us in force and destroyed the mission, I think that I could have rebuilt it. But they didn't need to. They just put one volunteer on the roof to fire a few shots from a rifle, and brought down the full weight of *American* fire-power on our heads. Our own people destroyed us. I felt that I couldn't stay any longer in a country where Americans were blindly destroying their own friends in order to save them. How can you save what you have first destroyed?"

I had no answer to that.

"Our head mission boy survived," Janet Deakin added softly. "Howard had baptized him when we first came to Vietnam, and he had been a staunch Christian and a loyal friend all through the war. But when he saw his friends die and the mission burn he decided that the Americans were wrong, and that we had been wrong, and that he had been wrong. He chose to go away and join the Viet Cong to try and avenge his friends, and we could not persuade him otherwise."

Howard nodded. "That was when I knew that we had failed, and that our lives had been wasted. Janet's health is getting frail, and I could not ask her to stay and start again. I knew it was time to go home."

15

He walked away to the end of the bridge, gripped the rail and stared at the passing shore.

Before she went to him Janet Deakin said quietly:

"I would have stayed to help him, but his heart was broken, so where was the point?"

CHAPTER THREE

BUTCHER departed from the bridge at the end of the noon watch, and left me to stand the two dog watches from four to eight p.m., and to see his ship safely out of the mouth of the Saigon River. It was dusk when our bows began to lift with the rising swell of the China Seas. The sun died in a gleam of red waves on the starboard bow, painting a brief funeral shroud of glory on the horizon. Then Ralph Yorke appeared to take the next watch.

In the dining saloon the off-duty officers and passengers were already seated when I arrived, and Hong had already served the soup. Butcher was predictably absent: he always preferred to eat in his cabin when the ship carried passengers, but Jean Pierre Lassalle was replendent in full uniform to occupy the Captain's seat at the head of the table.

Our Chief Engineer was happily situated between our two lady passengers like a thorny old hobgoblin between two roses. Lin Chi sat on his left, again looking exquisite in her traditional costume; while on his right Evelyn Ryan had changed into a primrose yellow dress with a pattern of autumn leaves. Ching sat beside Evelyn looking quite pleased with himself, while David Kee, our radio operator and Ching's close friend, sat in the next prized seat beside Lin Chi. A space had been left for me between the Deakins, and, to my surprise, the old monk.

"Bonjour, Monsieur Chief Officer!" Jean Pierre was in a fine mood. "Welcome to our table. Have you met all of our guests?"

"I believe so," I said, and smiled acknowledgements all round as Hong drew back my chair.

The old monk looked up into my face as I sat down and there was a twinkle of amusement in his eye. If he was out of place here, alone in his yellow robe, then presumably he did not notice, for he sat placidly enough with his hands resting in his lap. If he had been more rotund, and with a few of his wrinkles smoothed away, he would have looked like the Buddha. In front of him there was nothing except a glass of clear water.

Jean Pierre introduced him.

"This is the venerable Thich Huynh Quoc."

"You did not expect to see me here." The old man smiled and revealed that he spoke slow but excellent English. "You know that the rules of my robe forbid me to eat after the hour of noon. But I do not partake of any food. My companions remain in their cabins, but it seemed impolite that we should all seclude ourselves from your company. If I explain our ways then you will understand, and there can be no offence. That is why I share your table."

"You are very welcome," I told him.

At the same time I thought it strange, for there would be all day tomorrow while the ship plodded south through the empty seas when he would have ample time to socialize and make his apologies.

"Huynh Quoc is the senior priest of the Buddhist delegation we are taking to Singapore."

Jean Pierre was telling me what I already knew, but it kept the conversation flowing while Hong cleared the soup plates.

"There is to be a big convention," the old monk said precisely. "Monks from all the countries of South East Asia, and from all sections of the Buddhist faith will attend. There will be monks from Ceylon, and Thailand and Burma and Cambodia, as well as monks from Laos and South Vietnam. That is why we have chosen a neutral capital. We hope that we shall be able to bring our different countries, and the different schools of Theravada and Mahayana Buddhism, closer together."

18

"Then I hope that your convention will be successful," I said.

He acknowledged that with a murmur of thanks and a polite bow.

Hong enquired quietly whether I wanted soup but I shook my head. "I'll start with the main course," I said. "It's the quickest way to catch up."

At the far end of the table Jean Pierre had turned his attention to Lin Chi.

"*Parlez-vous français, mademoiselle?*"

"*Oui!*" Lin Chi smiled at him, "But I think that perhaps our companions do not, so we should speak in English."

David Kee was gallant. "Any language in which you speak would be music," he said.

"Then I shall speak English."

"Ah, but *français* is my native tongue." Jean Pierre sighed tragically. "It has been so long since I have heard it."

"*Pauvre Monsieur,*" Lin Chi laughed gently. "When we are alone, then I shall speak French with you. Then it will not be impolite."

"A promise," Jean Pierre said. "I shall hold you to it."

He slanted a rakish eyebrow at her, and I suspected that at any moment he would start singing "Thank Heaven, for Little Girls!" That was his usual party piece.

Hong forestalled him by serving slices of beef fried in oyster sauce with braised mushrooms and sweet green beans on white rice. Our galley staff were masters in the art of Cantonese cuisine.

"This is delicious," Evelyn Ryan said as she tasted it. "I must have the recipe."

"No can do," I answered. "Red hot pincers wouldn't draw a recipe out of Hong."

"I love eastern dishes. Does he always serve Chinese food?"

"Not always, the Captain insists on a few English meals. Tonight he's showing off for the passengers."

Hong hovered in the background, his face a golden

19

beam. Conversation became sparse as we enjoyed our food, while the old monk sipped his glass of water alone in pensive contemplation. Ching and David Kee were having a field day in passing condiments and exchanging smiles with our two fair guests.

I was hungry, but after a few minutes Jean Pierre remembered that he was filling in as host for the Captain. He paused to address himself to the Deakins.

"You are church people, I believe. Have you been preaching in Vietnam?"

"We are from a Catholic Mission Society," Howard Deakin corrected him mildly. "We ran a small mission school in the Central Highlands."

"That must have been very difficult."

Deakin nodded. He was not prepared to repeat the full story to the whole company, but he must have felt that it would be rude to refuse to answer.

"We tried to preach the Gospel, but in the past few years we have had so much work trying to help the sick and starving that there has barely been time to open a Bible. And the Viet Cong terrorized the local Vietnamese. They were afraid to become baptized and accept our teaching."

"Perhaps they were not so much afraid, but had no need of your faith," Huynh Quoc said equally mildly. "The Vietnamese people have had their own faith for eighteen centuries before you came; their faith in the Eightfold Path, and the teachings of Buddha."

Deakin hesitated and looked at him uncertainly.

"All people need the True Faith," he said, "the knowledge of the Love of Our Lord Jesus Christ."

"Another Master of Compassion," the old monk admitted. "But He is a part of Western culture. He is your faith, and it is your Western people who need him. He is not part of Asia. He spoke in your language, while Gotama Buddha spoke in ours."

"There is only one God, and only one language of God," Deakin said. "It is our duty to spread the Word."

"There are many Paths to ascend a Mountain. Your Jesus Christ pointed to one, while Gotama Buddha showed another. We who humbly follow must help to open the eyes of those who see no Path, but why circle the Mountain to steal men who are on other Paths? There is only the one Summit, where we must all unite."

"There is only one God, and we must carry the message of His name."

Deakin leaned forward to make his point. His eyes blinked behind his spectacles and I felt sorry for him. His beliefs must have been badly shaken by his past experiences, and he was not really fit to face a stiff theological argument.

"Your Catholic missionaries first brought your message to Vietnam four hundred years ago," Hyunh Quoc reminded him gently. "Then we were a peaceful land, ruled by our mandarin scholars and praying to Buddha. Your missionaries paved the way for the French colonialists, and their inheritors, the Americans—and now my country is a dying battlefield, laid waste by fire, and bombs and sprays of chemical poisons. Is that what your Jesus Christ desired of you?"

"We cannot know the Ways of God," Deakin insisted. "And besides, it was the Communists who started this war. They tried to take over your country."

"The Viet Cong have no napalm, and no bombs, and no chemical poisons," said the old monk. "And also they are Vietnamese, they are a part of our people. I cannot understand how your people can see *them* as foreign invaders on our soil!"

"But they terrorize your people who are not Communist. They threaten your Freedom!"

Huynh Quoc smiled with deep sadness, and his fingers plucked gently at the folds of his robe.

"There is only one freedom that is of any value, and that is the freedom for a man to find his own salvation. And that salvation is the Enlightment that lies within, and no other man can take that away from him."

"But you are not allowed to worship in a Communist state."

"A monk does not need to worship, only to meditate."

"They will give you no peace for meditation either."

Again the sad smile, the gentle reminder.

21

"So far it has only been the Diem Government, who were supported by the Americans, who have been the only ones to attack and close all the pagodas."

"Enough," I said. They were disputing in good temper but it was time to intervene. "I think we should change the subject away from religion and politics. It's too controversial for this part of the world."

"But it was interesting." Evelyn Ryan protested.

I agreed, but Deakin had had the foundations of his faith knocked about too badly, and I did not want to expose him to any more.

"There are other interesting topics," I suggested. "Let's find something else."

Evelyn looked at me angrily, resenting my interference, but I was rewarded by a brief flicker of gratitude from the bowed eyes of Janet Deakin.

"As you wish," Huynh Quoc said politely. "But let me say that I do not favour the Communists. I can merely see that it must be inevitable that they will take over Vietnam when the Americans withdraw, and so it seems better to come to terms with them now—while there is still something of my homeland left."

He fell silent, and sipped at his glass of water while the rest of us concluded our meal.

Hong served ice cream and then coffee before Jean Pierre decided to break the peace.

"I have thought of an interesting topic," he remarked, and he turned to Evelyn Ryan with a gallant gesture of his hand. "*Mademoiselle,* let us talk about you."

"About me!" she looked startled.

"Why yes. We know nothing about you except that you are beautiful to look upon. You must tell us more."

"Don't flatter me. I'm just an ordinary American girl."

"There is no such thing as an ordinary girl in any nationality. They all have their own charm, their own special attraction."

"You are an old rogue."

Jeanne Pierre beamed. He loved to be called such names.

"And anyway, I am just an ordinary American girl. I went to high school, and I went to college." She touched her fingers self consciously to her nose and laughed. "I still haven't gotten rid of all my freckles."

"They are adorable freckles," Jean Pierre assured her.

"You don't fool me one little bit," she retorted with a smile. "Anyway I studied history and sociology, and finally took a secretarial course. That's all."

"And why were you in Saigon?" Ching asked her.

"I was working as a secretary."

"Such a dangerous place to be a secretary," David Kee added his own bland smile.

She explained. "I was working with an American cultural research project."

They were all smiles and I tried to get into the act.

"It sounds like a cover for a branch of the CIA."

Evelyn Ryan stopped smiling and glared at me. A little pocket of cold silence wrapped up the table.

"That wasn't very intelligent," she said at last.

"I'm sorry." The joke had fallen flat and there was nothing to do except apologize for it.

"Our project was to research into the traditional ways of Vietnamese life," she continued firmly for my benefit. "We needed to correlate our findings so that US aid could be administered with as little damage as possible to the existing culture."

"I see," I said lamely.

I was feeling suitably abashed, but Lin Chi gave me compensation with a warmly sympathetic smile.

CHAPTER FOUR

On my way back to my cabin I lingered by the starboard rail. The *Shantung* was making her regular twelve knots and barely disturbing the dark swell of the waves. The night sky sparkled in all its cosmic glory, and it was several moments before I realized that I had a companion.

"You were so peaceful," Lin Chi said when I turned towards her. "I did not wish to speak and disturb you."

"That's all right." I smiled and made a grand gesture. "Please share my stars. I give them all to you."

"You are a poet," she laughed. "I find it hard to imagine that you are such a bully as Miss Ryan has described."

"She saw me in a bad moment."

"Yet you have the unhappy ability to continue to annoy her."

She was teasing, playing an oriental game with a bland face. I smiled awkwardly and said nothing.

"Miss Ryan likes your Second Officer," she said idly.

"Ralph has a certain charm,"

She looked to the bridge. "He is taking care of the ship?"

I nodded and wished that I had Ralph's easy manner with women. Her profile was smooth, shadowed loveliness as she stood close beside me, and I searched for the right topic to keep her there.

While I was still searching she went on:

"Your Captain did not dine with us tonight. I hope that he is not ill."

"Captain Butcher is in excellent health," I assured her. "Unfortunately he has no hair on his head, and so he

24

does not like to be seen without his cap. When we have passengers aboard he cannot wear his cap in the dining saloon, and so he prefers to eat in his cabin."

I spoke solemly and caused her to laugh.

"The poor Captain! But the little man who took his place was very nice. He has a sense of humour."

"That was Jean Pierre, our Chief Engineer."

"I promised to speak French with him." She suddenly remembered. "Alone!"

"Jean Pierre would be terrified if you kept that promise. He will be happier playing chess with the Captain, and drinking pink gins."

"You are trying to keep me for yourself."

"Of course."

We shared the same smile and I asked:

"Why are you travelling to Singapore?"

"To get away from Vietnam." She spoke simply and it was a good enough reason. She paused and then observed: "But you are asking me to tell you about myself, and you are too polite to question me directly. That is the Asian way. It is unlike the ways of the West."

"I have been in the East for a long time."

She turned and gazed down at the dark sea, reflecting and gathering her thoughts, and then she began to explain quietly.

"My home was in Hue. It was the old imperial capital of Vietnam, built on the left bank of the Perfume River. It was a very beautiful old city of walls and moats and palaces. I was a student there, I studied medicine. My mother died when I was small but my father was a very learned man. He was a scholar and a professor of languages, an intellectual man, and one of the last of the old mandarins. We had a very nice home, with a small patio and lotus pools in the garden."

She lingered over the memory and I waited for her to continue.

"Finally the Viet Cong captured Hue during the big Tet Offensive. The Americans would not let them keep the city and they came with tanks and planes to win it back. It took them four weeks to drive out the Viet

Cong and to do it they had to raze Hue to the ground. I spent those four weeks hiding in a cellar. It was more terrible than you could imagine. When we emerged our house was just a pile of rubble—like the rest of the city. Thousands of people were dead. When the Viet Cong had 'liberated' us we still had a city, but after the Americans had 'liberated' us we had nothing."

"I'm sorry," I said softly. It was the second time that I had said that today, and the second time that I realized what a totally inadequate thing it was to say.

She did not elaborate any further and I did not press her. She looked up at last and said:

"That is why I am going to Singapore. If they will let me stay then perhaps I can continue my studies there."

"I am sure they will let you stay in Singapore."

We became silent again. A night like this one was made to be prolonged by long pauses. We stood close, almost touching.

"How long have you been in the East?"

"Fifteen years." I smiled. "But you were inviting me to talk about myself, and you are too polite to ask me directly. It is the Asian way."

She laughed. She looked very desirable then.

"I came out from London to join this same company as an officer cadet. I made my first trip on a very old ship called the *Honan*. She rolled terribly even on a calm sea like this one, and I was very seasick and fell down all the ladders. I soon got over it and found my sea legs, and I was Third Officer when the *Honan* cracked a propeller shaft and had to be towed away for scrap. Then I came aboard the *Shantung* as Second Officer and I've been here ever since. Now I'm First Mate."

"That is the same as First Officer?"

"The same."

"And next you will be Captain?"

"That's the next step."

She turned her hip to the rail and looked up at me.

"Don't you miss your home country?"

"There isn't much to miss. The weather there is grey and wet, and I've got no ties. I can get leave to go home for a few weeks every nine months, but now I never take it."

"You have no family?"

"Only one brother, but he's a different kind of man from me. He works in a bank, closed up all day with accounts and figures and papers. I need the open sea. We had nothing in common."

"Have you a special woman in Singapore?"

"No."

"In Hong Kong perhaps?"

"No. I'm not that lucky."

"If you do not have one woman who is important, then you must have many women who are not!"

I shrugged. "Maybe."

"Many women?"

"A few." I could only give a casual answer to that.

I wasn't sure whether she was merely teasing me or whether I was being seduced. There was no moonlight, but the starlight was bright and romantic enough, and I had heard all about that old tropical heat. However, I had assumed that it only worked on bored young husband hunters on the big cruise ships, or the young wives bored with their husbands. Asian women were better behaved, and I wouldn't expect them to be affected.

Lin Chi was gazing at me boldly.

"Have you ever known a Vietnamese woman?"

"Not really. Perhaps we should get better acquainted."

"Perhaps we should."

It was an invitation, and yet she turned away and looked idly out to sea. I remembered an old Asian proverb and waited. A man does not capture a butterfly by grabbing it in a clumsy fist.

After a while she folded her arms across her breasts and looked up at me again.

"The night turns cool I think."

"Only the breeze. In my cabin there is no breeze, and I have a new Japanese record player and some classical records. Do you like western classical music?"

"Yes, but I will not come to your cabin." She smiled at my disappointment and then her hand moved along

27

the rail to touch my own. "You may come to my cabin—in an hour."

"Why must we wait an hour?"

"Do not ask questions."

I remembered the proverb, and I could not risk losing my butterfly now.

She smiled again, and then she withdrew and I was alone.

I reflected on the strange twists of fortune, and especially the unpredictable behaviour of women, and then at last I turned away and made a quiet tour of the ship. The decks were deserted and I ascended to the bridge to find Ralph Yorke yawning with boredom. He looked at me curiously and I explained that I was just stretching my legs before I turned in for the night.

There was a faint light in the radio room and I found David Kee tinkering into one of his pieces of equipment with a screwdriver. He glanced up as I looked in.

"You're working late, David?"

He nodded. "This receiver needs adjusting, and it is so much cooler to work at night. I take long siestas in the day."

"You have a wonderful life. The number of messages we send out and receive must take up about two per cent of your time!"

He laughed and I left him to his work.

There was another bar of light showing from the Captain's cabin, and I passed close enough to hear the clink of a bottle neck against glasses through the open port.

"That's a new gambit, Old Frog," I heard Butcher say. "Have you cheated and bought another new book on the game?"

I smiled wryly and moved on. Everything was normal.

My wristwatch showed that exactly sixty minutes had elapsed when I knocked lightly on the door of cabin number four. I did not intend to exhibit any impatience, but neither did I have any desire to keep my lady waiting.

The door opened and Lin Chi was smiling at me, she still wore the bronze-coloured tunic over the white silk trousers, and looked slightly nervous. She stood aside to let me in and then quietly closed the door.

"Hello, Johnny."

"Hello, Lin Chi."

She waited awkwardly, standing close, and I drew her closer. Her black eyes gazed up into mine from beneath delicately arched brows, and then her slim arms came up behind my neck. I kissed her upon the lips as though she was fragile china. There was something in her manner that told me that my butterfly must not be crudely crushed.

When she lowered her lips I kissed the tip of her nose, and then her smooth forehead, and then the smooth black silkiness of her hair. My fingers found the tiny bow of black ribbon that tied her pony tail and slowly pulled it free. The black waves of her hair cascaded over my hand. She looked up at me and smiled, and then drew away.

"I have some wine," she said. "It is French wine, and very expensive in Vietnam."

There was something curously naïve about her, as though she was playing this scene from an old book she had read, or an old film she had once seen. She produced a bottle of *Château Ausone,* the label faded and stained with age, and invited me to open it.

I pulled the cork for her and watched her pour two fine cut glasses. She must have brought her own, for we had no glassware like that on board the ship. She handed me one of the glasses of wine and then we sat on the edge of the bed while she made a toast.

"To you, Johnny."

"No, Lin Chi, to you—may you find peace and happiness in Singapore."

She hesitated, as though I had touched a nerve that gave her pain. She raised her glass and sipped.

"The wine is sweet."

"Your lips were sweeter."

29

She smiled faintly. Now that her hair was loose it was as though she had been transformed from a woman to a child. Some of her poise was gone and she looked defenceless.

"Have you really known very many women, Johnny?"

"Some," I said. "But not many. And none like you."

"Will you be gentle with me, Johnny?"

"Very gentle. As gentle as I know how."

I set my glass down and took hers from her hand. She came close and I kissed her again. Her heart was trembling against my hand, and again I caressed her long sleek hair. She lay back on the bed and my lips touched her cheek. The high collar of her tunic was in my way and I felt for the buttons.

"Put the light off, Johnny."

It was a whispered plea and I obeyed, reluctantly because she was beautiful and I wanted to look at her. In the darkness she helped me find the buttons, and slipped out of the close tunic. Her skin was cool and smooth to my touch and I removed her bra. It had been a long time and the blood began to pound through my veins. Lin Chi became frightened and began to struggle.

"Please, Johnny. Please—not so rough."

"It's all right." I became still with an effort, and then moved my hand to stroke back her hair. "It's all right," I repeated. "I won't hurt you."

She still trembled, but after a while she turned her head and her lips brushed my hand. I bowed my head to kiss her cheek and then she gave me her lips again. I kissed and caressed her tenderly for what seemed a very long time before she finally allowed me to remove her white silk trousers.

There was enough starlight filtering through the curtained port for us to each distinguish the other's silhouette in the darkness, and she turned her head and closed her eyes while I undressed in turn. When I leaned back to her she was huddled close with her face turned away. She was a strange mixture of reluctance and boldness. I could have forced her with ease, but I had promised to be gentle. I stroked the soft white curves of her body,

30

dimly visible in the starlight, keeping my hands feather light. I kissed the tiny lobe of her ear, her cheek, and then her mouth moved freely to find mine once more. She opened her arms to me, and then her whole body.

"Oh, Johnny!"

She was a captive white bird, closed in the muscled cage of my arms. She trembled and her heart was beating fit to burst through her straining breast. I stopped her entreaty with a kiss and fought my own desire in an effort to remain gentle.

She was a virgin, it was so obvious now, and she cried out under my kiss. We were one, but I soothed her again, and then she clung to me tightly as we began the slow motion that carried us up to the stars. It was as though the tides of space lifted us into a galaxy of delights, rising and falling but ever ascending into waves of sparkling rapture. The star-heat enveloped us, and penetrated us, and then broke within us. It took a long time because I was exercising all my powers of self control in an effort not to hurt her, but finally they were swamped in the white, bursting, brain-lost heat and I had to hurt her. She stiffened and engulfed me and cried out in the fiery sweetness where pain and ecstasy, and man and woman are all one.

Then slowly we descended, and the stars dimmed and steadied into stillness, and we became two separate people once again.

I knew that I was heavy and moved my weight, and for a moment I lay wondering. I had just received a precious gift and I did not know why. Lin Chi lay with her face turned away from me and was very still, and I rested my hand on her shoulder.

"Lin Chi," I said softly. "Look at me."

She was silent, and then her voice muffled against the pillow.

"Why, Johnny?"

"Because it isn't finished when the physical part is over. You need me now as much as I needed you a moment ago."

She turned slowly, hesitantly, and I took her in my arms again. I kissed the tears away from her closed

31

eyes, and then she lowered her head and pressed her face against my chest. She lay very small and cold and still, and I knew she was still crying. I continued to caress her. I believed then that she was crying because it had been too soon, and because she feared that I would take it too lightly.

We still lay together when the explosion hit the *Shantung* like an almighty blow above the heart. The blast was deafening and the old freighter rocked and shuddered from stem to stern. It sounded and felt as though we had been torpedoed, except that a torpedo would have struck below the waterline and this impact had been too high and too close.

I catapulted out of the bed like a stung jackrabbit, snapped on the light and lunged for the door. I remembered that I was stark naked and paused to grab for my pants, and then I froze in a new numb shock of amazement.

Lin Chi was sitting up on the bed and with her left hand she held a sheet up to her small breasts. The tear stains were still on her anguished face, and in her hand there was a small black automatic that was aimed at my heart.

"Please, Johnny," she begged. "Please remain still. Do not make me have to kill you."

CHAPTER FIVE

I STRAIGHTENED up slowly and stared into her eyes. I realized that I had been duped and I felt disgusted with my own stupidity. A few moments ago I had been making love to her, not just stealing sex but really making love to her. And now it was all revealed as nothing but a charade and she was threatening to kill me. What a stupid fool I was!

I could hear shouts and startled voices breaking out all over the reeling *Shantung*. The ship had been rudely awakened and it sounded as though every man aboard was running frantically to and fro. However, I remained still. Not because she had ordered me to do so but because the answers were here, behind the black nose of the gun with Lin Chi. I tasted bile and bitterness in the back of my throat and demanded harshly:

"Just what the hell is happening?"

She blinked and said simply:

"We are taking over your ship."

"And who the hell are *we*?"

"Please, Johnny—do not ask me questions. Not now."

Another tear trickled down her smooth cheek but I ignored it, it was just another crocodile tear. The meaning of so many things hit me like a succession of blows. Lin Chi's subtle interrogation: was the Second Officer on the bridge? Where was the Captain? The hour's delay she had begged to pass on her information. My invitation to her cabin, the waiting wine, my seduction. Her boldness and reluctance and the tears. Now they all fitted together.

"Who is taking over my ship?"

The words snarled out of my throat and I took an

angry step towards her. She dropped the sheet and clasped both hands around her automatic.

"Please, Johnny, stay back."

Her knuckle was white around the trigger, and so I stayed back. I looked down at the gun and said bitterly:

"I suppose that was under the pillow all the time?"

"Yes, Johnny." She nodded her head. "That was why it had to be in my cabin and not yours." Her face was ready to dissolve into more weeping. "Johnny, you should not have been so gentle with me. I know that I asked you to be gentle but it was not what I deserved. Now it has made things so difficult."

"I'll bet it has." I almost spat the words at her.

I glared into her eyes and she returned my gaze, unhappy but not flinching. At least she knew better than to take her eyes or the gun away from me for even a bare second. In that moment I could have strangled her with that loose black hair.

Abruptly there came a crash of rifle fire from the direction of the bridge, filling the emptiness where the echoes of that first violent explosion had died away. Lin Chi started up with fright and her head twisted briefly towards the sound, and I risked the gun and jumped her.

I knocked the gun aside as my body crashed down on hers and pinned her to the bed. She shrieked but the gun did not go off. I caught her wrist and twisted savagely as she squirmed like a naked wildcat beneath me. The sheet ripped and tore between us and the gun clattered to the floor. She tried to bite and her nails raked at my bare back and shoulders. Her legs thrashed and I had to yank her head back by the hair and smash the back of my hand across her face. There was no time and I was in no mood to be gentle now.

Some of the fight went out of her and I clamped my hand over her mouth to stop her from screaming. She wasn't trying to take over the ship on her own and that meant that she had friends who would come running to her calls. Her eyes were black pools of dilated fear and she writhed again as I found the silk trousers she had discarded and knotted them crudely around her mouth to keep her quiet.

I turned her over without ceremony and secured her wrists despite her struggles. My necktie was the nearest thing to hand for that purpose and for good measure I dragged her to the edge of the bed and passed a couple of loops around the cold water tap of the nearby basin before tying the final knots. It left her hoisted half off the bed by her arms but at least she wouldn't be moving very far unless she was strong enough to tear the whole fitting off the bulkhead.

She was having a damned good try and making muffled squeals through her gag but I left her to it. I had no more time to waste. The shooting had ceased on the bridge but pandemonium still reigned aboard the ship. I grabbed for my trousers, hauled them on, and in the same instant there came a sharp knock on the door.

I snatched up the automatic from the deck and threw the cabin door wide before the Vietnamese voice that followed the knock had completed its sharp note of enquiry. One of the young monks stood there, still showing a modest bare shoulder through his yellow robe, but no longer a pacific follower of the Buddha.

In his hands he held a combat rifle, the Russian pattern AK–47 that was much favoured by the Viet Cong.

I grabbed the rifle by the barrel and heaved him in bodily through the door. As he stumbled forward I used the automatic in my right hand as an improvised knuckle duster and slugged him across the jaw with all my strength. He went down like a yellow rice sack and as he fell I wrenched the rifle out of his hands.

I let him lie on the deck and paused only to buckle my belt and thrust Lin Chi's little automatic into my waistband. The combat rifle fitted my hands better for a battle.

I stepped out into the passageway, bare chested and in bare feet, and heard the raised, protesting voices of Howard Deakin and Evelyn Ryan. Their cabins were just around a bend in the passageway and it sounded as though they were being rooted out at gunpoint.

For one brief second I hesitated. The key point for

commanding the ship was the bridge, but the rifle shots from that direction had ceased and I suspected that in one way or another the issue was settled. The combat rifle in my hands could change all that, but it would do me no good to recapture the bridge only to surrender it again while our passengers were forced to stand as hostages with guns at their heads.

I had to make an instant choice and I closed the door of number four quietly behind me to seal off the sound of Lin Chi's struggles, and then turned towards the bend in the passageway and the remaining cabins. I was temporarily turning my back on the bridge, but I had decided to first tackle the job that was nearest to hand. Perhaps it would prove to be the wrong choice, but a decision gave me a fifty per cent better chance of being right than no decision at all.

"What's happening?" I heard Evelyn Ryan say angrily. "Look, you can't come into my cabin. I'm not even—"

I turned the corner with my shoulders to the bulkhead and the rifle levelled. The corridor was empty but the doors of both the nearer cabins were wide open. Evelyn Ryan appeared in the doorway of number three, the nearer cabin, and she had obviously been pushed. She was wearing nothing but a flimsy nightdress and an expression of freckled indignation. She stumbled, saw me standing there and gaped.

There was a movement of yellow and a second robed monk appeared behind her. He too held a levelled rifle but it was pointed at the American girl. I sprang forward before her startled look betrayed me.

I could have shot him, but I remembered that there had been eight monks altogether and I didn't want to bring his little yellow friends buzzing around my ears. Instead I used my rifle to dash his weapon away, one downward, sweeping blow with the barrel which smashed it from his hands, and then hooking the butt round to drive it hard into his middle. He folded up and I cut him viciously across the side of his exposed neck with the stiffened edge of my palm. He hit the deck like another sack of rice.

36

I was on a winning streak and I didn't stop. I stepped over his crumpled form and ran on down the passageway. Half a dozen long strides took me to the doorway of cabin number two and I turned inside and surprised another monk. He was standing with his back to me and his rifle covering the Deakins. The missionary was sitting on the edge of his bed in his pyjamas, his round face pale and uncertain as he groped for his spectacles. Janet Deakin was huddled beside him, grey and bewildered, in a nightdress that was somewhat longer and more respectable than the one that Evelyn Ryan had been wearing.

The monk started to turn and I jabbed my rifle barrel in his ribs. Three made the jackpot for I felt that the others must be attacking the bridge, and I did not want to give any further exhibitions of violence in front of a frail and frightened old lady.

"Hold it," I snapped curtly. "Just hold it right there."

He turned his head to look at me, a hard, smooth Asian face with startled slits for eyes. Maybe he didn't understand my words but he knew what I meant, and he went white around the gills.

Deakin found his spectacles and put them on, and then he stood up and gingerly took the combat rifle from the monk's uncertain hands.

"What's happening?" he asked me. "What was that explosion?"

"I don't know yet," I said briefly. "I think they're trying to hijack the ship!"

"But—"

"Watch him," I ordered, and started to turn away. Time was vital.

Evelyn Ryan appeared to block the doorway. She seemed to have recovered her composure pretty fast, and in her hands she held the rifle that had been dropped by the second monk.

"What on earth is going on?" she demanded.

"I'll tell you when I find out."

I pushed past her, and ran back up the passageway and grabbed the fallen monk by his heels. I heaved him roughly back into the Deakins' cabin.

They stared at me with uncomprehending faces. The captive monk who was conscious merely glared.

"You'd better give me those."

I took the two spare combat rifles and slung them both across my shoulders. Evelyn released hers reluctantly.

"Do you need them all?"

"If I can reach my crew I can issue them out." I pulled Lin Chi's automatic out of my waistband and offered it to her. "Do you think you can hold this instead and just watch our little pal here?"

She gave me a suddenly strange smile.

"I think I can manage that."

"Okay, I'll leave you to it. I have to get to the bridge."

I gave them all the best that I could manage in the way of a reassuring smile, trying to fool them that Chief Officer Steele was in command of the situation, and then I hurried out. I closed the door on them and knew that with three monks down I still had five to go. The night's work was far from over.

It would be pointless checking the other cabins, for I knew that the remaining monks would not be there. They would be on the bridge but the odds were better balanced now. I had two spare rifles and perhaps I could arm Ho Wan or Ching, if either of them were still free and able to fight.

I slipped out on to the open deck and then ran lightly to the companionway that led to the boatdeck above. Here there was no one to stop me and my bare feet made no sound on the caulked boards. I ran faster when I saw the ominous red glow that radiated up to the night sky.

I took the ascending rungs three at a time, one hand on the rail and the other gripping a rifle. As I reached the top I stopped and flinched back from the heat, and now there was no longer any doubt in my mind as to the source of the explosion. The radio room was a shambles and a blaze of fire.

There was no one else on the boatdeck and I sprinted towards the scene with a new sickness in my heart. The blackened door was sagging on its buckled hinges and I threw it back. Inside the flames were roaring and licking up the walls and the red tongues scorched my chest and face. The sweat began to stream out of me and I had to lift my bare arm to shield my eyes. There was nothing left of our radio equipment, neither the main transmitter and receiver or the reserve set. All those carefully polished and adjusted knobs and dials and wavebands were gone, half melted into a heap of shattered glass and steel. And on top of the collapsed tables in the midst of all the mess sprawled a mutilated figure that could only be David Kee.

It was cooler to work at night, he had said. He would sleep in the heat of the day. Poor David, now he would sleep for ever.

I forced my way inside and crouched beside him. His cap had been blown off and his face was a mask of blood, deeply embedded with flying glass from the broken valves. Whatever had caused the explosion had occurred between his tables of equipment and the far bulkhead. A large, fiery hole had been torn in the bulkhead itself, and the disintegrating parts of the radio sets had been blasted full into his face.

So the explosion had been inside the radio room, some kind of a time bomb perhaps, and suddenly I knew with instinctive certainty when it had been placed in position. This morning when that net had been cut and that damned clumsy winch driver had all but dropped the falling cargo on my head. He hadn't been so clumsy after all. He had known exactly what he was doing. The commotion he had caused had brought Butcher out from the bridge, and it would have drawn David from the radio room if he had been there. Ample time for someone to slip in and plant a pre-set bomb.

I reached down and got a grip on David's blood-soaked collar with my free hand. He had died instantly but I could not leave him there. Even though my lungs were choking and my eyebrows and the hairs on my chest were burning I had to drag him out on to the open deck.

He was a sailor and a brother officer, and the least I

could do was to ensure that his body was buried honourably at sea.

Those extra rifles across my back snagged in the doorway and almost trapped me as I struggled backwards. I cursed and swallowed more blistered air and black smoke that burned in my throat. I got out and dragged David clear but for the moment I was helpless. I knelt over him fighting for breath as the roof of the radio room collapsed in a new blaze of fire and a cascade of sparks, and through streaming eyes I saw Butcher emerge from his cabin and head for the bridge.

Only a few minutes had elapsed since the initial explosion and the short burst of rifle shots that had followed. I had been moving fast but Butcher looked as though he was drunk and it had taken him time to find his clothes. He was ramming his cap on to his head and moving at an unsteady run.

I shouted to him but the hoarse croak that came out of my raw throat was blotted out by the roaring of the fire behind me. Butcher reached the companionway to the bridge and rushed upwards, shouting as he went.

"Mister Yorke! *Mister Yorke, where are you?*"

I knew that Ralph was no longer in command of the bridge. If he had been then steps would have been taken to control that fire before I arrived. I tried to straighten up but slipped and fell in a pool of David's blood.

A figure moved on the silent bridge, the blur of another yellow robe. Butcher was at the top of the companionway and the monk moved swiftly into the firelight to intercept him. There was no need to waste ammunition. The combat rifle in the monk's hand was reversed and he met Butcher's charge by driving the butt solidly against the Captain's chest. Butcher fell back, a fat, ungainly figure somersaulting heavily down the companionway. He bellowed out frantically as he sailed downwards, and then hit the deck with an almighty thump that made me wince. He screamed with pain at the impact.

Reason snapped. I was blistered and hurt and I had a dead shipmate at my feet. This was *my* ship and that sloppy old alcoholic was for all his faults another of *my*

40

shipmates. He was *my* Captain. I sighted the combat rifle in my hands without any further thought, and squeezed the trigger.

The AK–47 was beautifully balanced, a light-weight automatic weapon that even a child could have handled. It was made that way because children could be trained into useful guerilla fighters. A short burst of bullets crashed out and the man in the yellow robe twitched round and was flung back out of my sight.

I knew that he was dead, four monks down and four to go, but still it had been a mistake. There were more intruders up on the bridge and they had a better defensive position than I had. An answering burst of fire gouged out a shower of splinters from the deck beside me but already I was scrambling aside. Even in that moment I didn't forget David and hauled him along with one hand as I ran for the protection of the smoke-stack. I ducked behind it as another crash of bullets ricocheted deafeningly off the steel plates.

I circled swiftly round to the starboard side of the boat deck, but again a burst of firing drove me back. I cursed and considered my next move. They had me pinned down and now it was impossible to get past the bridge and link up with the Bo'sun and the crew who were undoubtedly trapped in the peak. I had two spare rifles and there was no one I could arm. Where the hell was Ching?

I risked showing my face again and exhanged more staccato bursts of automatic fire. It cost me half a clip of ammunition but a least it enabled me to count the answering flashes on the bridge. There were three men up there which meant that there was only one monk left unaccounted for.

I withdrew, thinking fast. Three monks to take care of myself and the passengers, four monks on the bridge, and one monk where? There was one other vital point and that was the engine room. One man on the high catwalk could cover Jean Pierre and his staff and take control there, and they had to control the engine room.

I made my decision. Forget the bridge for a while and get down to the engine room. If I could add another monk to my bag and release the engineers then I could arm enough men to re-take the bridge.

I turned away confidently, a positive course of action in mind. But I was confident too soon and all my calculations were hopelessly wrong. I had been crouching behind the smokestack, and as I turned I all but stubbed out my eye on the black barrel of an automatic. It was held in a gnarled, ancient hand, with skin the texture of brown parchment, and behind it was the troubled and sorrowful face of Huynh Quoc.

"Please, Mister Steele," the old man said earnestly. "Do not make me kill you. It will cause me bad *kharma* for which I must suffer in a future rebirth."

It was the second time tonight that I had been begged to behave myself from behind the barrel of a gun. I didn't give a damn about his *kharma,* but a bullet from that automatic only had to travel three inches to blow my brains out and again I had no alternative. Bitterly I lowered the rifle.

I saw Lin Chi behind him. He had released her and now she was fully dressed. She came past him and took the combat rifle out of my hands, and then stepped back to point it at my chest. Her face was still sad.

"You should have listened to me, Johnny," she said.

I had nothing to say to her and she raised her voice and shouted to the bridge in Vietnamese. Another voice answered and there was a brief exchange of words, and then she motioned me out on to the open deck.

Huynh Quoc had been half kneeling like an old yellow gnome behind me. He straightened up and withdrew, allowing me to rise in turn. Swallowing my gall I walked out towards the bridge.

Butcher was still lying at the foot of the companionway, groaning and twisting in agony. On the port side the radio room still blazed and cast pools of flickering light. I looked up and saw an arm trailing over the edge of the bridge with spots of blood dripping gently from the lifeless fingers. On the jacket sleeve were two gold rings of the Second Officer.

CHAPTER SIX

THERE was nothing that I could do for Ralph, and so I knelt down beside Butcher. I could smell the reek of gin on his breath and he was sweating profusely. His normally red face was pale and glistening, almost white, and his eyes and lips were screwed tightly shut as though he was fighting to keep his pain inside. His right leg was twisted at a grotesque angle, broken below the knee. His cap had rolled away to reveal the stark baldness of his head, and for the moment the only thing that I could do for him was to replace it. The *Shantung* carried no regular doctor, but Jean Pierre had a smattering of medical knowledge.

I straightened up and turned on Lin Chi and the old monk, but a patter of light sandals on the companionway interrupted me before I even got started. I looked up as another of the younger monks descended swiftly from the bridge. He too carried a combat rifle and his face was a slit-eyed mask of viciousness. I had bowed to all the monks as they came aboard, and I wondered how I had ever been dumb enough to believe that this face belonged to the yellow robe. He stopped two steps up from the deck so that his face was level with mine and surprised me again by speaking angry English:

"So, it was the Chief Officer who gave us all this trouble. You have killed one of my friends!"

"And you have cold-bloodedly murdered two of mine."

I wanted to pluck him off the companionway and break his rotten little neck, but the combat rifles held me back. Two more armed men moved into view at the top of the companionway, and for a moment my anger was forgotten as I stared towards them. They were not wearing the yellow robe, and I was certain that I had not seen them before.

Slowly I realized that I had not been fighting the eight monks alone. The odds had been greater than that.

"This is Section Leader Thang." Huynh Quoc said behind me. He is in command of this guerilla unit."

"I don't give a damn whether he's Ho Chi Minh, Chairman Mao, or Father Christmas," I told him bluntly. "I'm still in command of this ship. I want the Chief Engineer brought up here to attend to the Captain. I want my Third Officer on deck. And I want my Bo'sun and enough of the duty watch to put out that fire. On the double!"

Huynh Quoc looked uncertain, but Section Leader Thang snapped back:

"You are no longer in command. I have captured this ship. I will give the orders."

"Then you can just repeat my orders," I told him harshly. I stabbed a finger towards the blazing radio room. "Other wise you'll have that fire out of control and the whole ship will burn."

Thang hesitated and both Huynh Quoc and Lin Chi started to argue with him in Vietnamese. Thang tightened his lips angrily, he resented any opposition or advice but at least he was not a fool. What needed to be done was as plain to him as it was to me. He waved the old man and the girl silent and then shouted curtly up to his men on the bridge. One of them answered and then vanished from sight, and I heard him scurrying down to the foredeck.

"The men you need will be brought here," Thang said. "Now give me the rifles you have stolen."

I still had the two spare combat rifles slung across my shoulders. I had almost forgotten them and I disentangled them one by one and handed them back. It was an issue on which I couldn't challenge him. He glared at me coldly as he passed the weapons up to his friend who remained on the bridge, and then demanded:

44

"What happened to the men from whom you stole these rifles?"

I didn't want to answer that. I remembered Evelyn Ryan and realized that I had placed her in a position of danger. If she attempted to resist this ugly little hoodlum with the puny automatic I had given her she would finish up dead. However Huynh Quoc knew all the answers.

"They are all alive," the old monk said. "One man is unconscious in Lin Chi's cabin, and the other two are being held by the American girl who has a small gun. I did not have time to release them. They will come to no harm and we can attend to them later."

He turned meaningful eyes towards the fire, and in the same moment Ching appeared in the light of the flames. He was walking unsteadily with his hands raised level with his shoulders, and behind him was a ragged Vietnamese with the inevitable AK–47 and a coolie hat. I recognized my old enemy the clumsy winch operator.

Ching looked white and sick and shaken.

"Mister Steele," he cried out in anguish. "They have killed David Kee."

I realized that he must have passed the body of his friend where I had dragged it clear and left it against the smoke-stack. They had been closer than brothers and I saw that there was bottled fury in his grief.

"I know that, Mister Ching," I said sharply. "They also killed the Second Officer and we can't afford any more dead men." I knew that I had to be cruel to be kind and work him hard in the next five minutes, otherwise he would explode blindly into open rebellion and get himself killed.

"Give me a hand with the hose," I ordered. "We have to control this fire."

I turned and hurried briskly to the long coil of hose that hung in its square wooden box against the ship's rail. The combat rifles all bristled and followed me, but then Thang gave a reluctant order in Vietnamese.

"No tricks," was all that he said warningly in English.

I ignored them all and Ching came to help me. Al-

45

ready we had left the fire for too long. The hose was swiftly unwound and Ching ran it out towards the fire while I coupled it up to the sea cock in the scuppers. I shouted a warning to Ching and then rapidly spun open the wheel valve. The hose writhed and stiffened and then a fierce jet of sea water gushed out of the heavy brass nozzle. Ching had braced himself and only staggered slightly as he directed it into the heart of the flames, and in the same moment part of the deck collapsed with a sudden roar and a burst of sparks. The burning debris fell through on to the deck below.

We now had a fire on two decks and spreading fast, and beyond what was left of the gutted radio room I could see that the first of the two port lifeboats was also wreathed in scarlet tongues. I was well aware that none of the regularly practised fire drill had been put into effect, and with Thang and his guerilla unit in uncertain control there was no hope that the crew would be allowed to move freely to close up the ports and ventilators to draught proof the ship. The fire had to be put out immediately or the *Shantung* would go up like a torch.

"Hold her steady!" I yelled to Ching who was already doing his best, and then headed at a run for the deck below. Thang followed me rapidly with his gun at my back, but half-way down the companionway I met Ho Wan coming up equally fast. Behind him was a group of half a dozen anxious Chinese seamen, and behind them three more ragged Vietnamese with levelled rifles.

There was dried blood caked thickly all down the side of the Bo'sun's face, a sure sign that he had put up a damned good fight, but now he acted as though he had not been hurt at all.

"Mister Steele. What happen?"

"The radio shack is burned out," I informed him crisply. "Get two of these men up on the boat deck to help the Third Officer. And get another hose going on the deck below. Move to it!"

"Aye, aye, sir!"

Wan turned and translated my orders in the same

breath, and at the same time hustled the crewmen down below again. The three armed guerillas scrambled aside to give them room but refused to lower their rifles. The sailors were scared but they could see the danger to the ship and Ho Wan urged them on. Here there was another hose boxed against the rail and two men frantically proceeded to get it into action. The port alleyway inside the rail leading to the stern of the ship was now blocked by a mass of fire.

I was on the Bo'sun's heel but as my feet hit the deck the cold barrel of Thang's rifle gouged in under my left ear.

"Enough," he said. "Let these men and your Third Officer see to the fire. You I do not trust. You will warn your friends that if they attempt to turn those very powerful water jets on my men then you, their Chief Officer, will die."

I swung around to argue with him, but those slit eyes told me that this time he was in no mood for argument. As he had foreseen those water jets would be almost as devastating as one of his own combat rifles if they were to be unexpectedly turned upon a man, and would have just as good a sweep effect. Section Leader Thang was a man who calculated possibilities and took no chances.

Ho Wan paused momentarily and looked back, his face gory and ominous in the glow of the flames, and his eyes weighing Thang's words.

"I have heard," he said.

"The Captain will also die," Thang added for good measure.

"I have heard," the Bo'sun repeated. "I will put out the fire."

He turned his back on us and strode forward, shouting out commands. Thang stood back from the companionway and prodded my neck again.

"Let us go back to the boatdeck."

I stayed for a minute, watching Ho Wan and satisfying myself that he needed no help. Then I nodded and climbed back up the steps. Thang followed me at a safe distance.

Ching was still wrestling alone with the heavy hose,

but as soon as Thang had followed me clear of the top of the comapnionway two of Wan's men came hurrying up to help. The sailors ran to Ching's side, and with two men to steady the gushing brass nozzle and the third to drag the hose where it was most needed they had the mobility to get the blaze under control.

From the deck below I heard the sizzling hiss of steam as the second hose spurted into operation.

The lifeboat was still burning, and although the fire was now being swiftly extinguished on both decks I had the sudden, bleak feeling that somewhere in the not too distant future the boats might yet be needed.

"Ching," I shouted. "Douse that lifeboat!"

Ching looked up, his face tight and glistening, and painted with a red glow in the violent heat. He spoke curtly to the man beside him and they turned the nozzle of the hose. The jet climbed higher and hit the burning boat hard enough to make it jump as it swung between the derricks. The surge of water washed away the licking flames and left only the blackened boards. Ching left the hose there for a moment and then brought it back to play around the red edges of the gaping hole where the radio room had been.

There was nothing else that I could do, except hope that the Bo'sun was winning his battle on the deck below. Thang had decided that I was not to be trusted, and in that I had to admit that he was right. I meant to take back the *Shantung* at the very first opportunity that came my way. In the meantime Thang wasn't letting me an inch out of his sight.

I walked back slowly to the foot of the bridge where Butcher still lay. Huynh Quoc was kneeling beside him and Lin Chi stood at the old monk's shoulder. They both looked up as I approached. For a moment I saw again the dead arm with the two gold rings that hung limply from the bridge, and I watched another small globule of blood trickle slowly down the extended index finger, swell, and then fall to the deck. Then I turned my eyes to Lin Chi. Her face was pale like that of a sick child. Her long black hair was still loose and some of the buttons of her hastily donned tunic were still un-done.

"Ralph Yorke was my friend," I said for her alone. "You helped to kill him. And David Kee, our radio operator—the Chinese boy who sat beside you at dinner, the one who smiled and made you laugh so much, and passed you the bloody salt!—he's dead too. He was working in the radio room when it blew up."

"Please, Johnny—" her lips trembled.

"I pulled him out of that fire—" I wasn't going to spare her anything. "—what was left of him. Why didn't you seduce him instead? If you had taken David to your cabin and wrapped your whore's legs around him you might have saved his life."

"Johnny, please!"

She bit her lip and turned away from me, hiding her face against her shoulder. I might have hesitated and eased up on her, but Thang intervened.

"Enough," he snapped. "Be silent."

I turned on him savagely.

"I haven't forgotten you. And I won't forget. You've signed your own death warrant by murdering two of my officers. Because if you need this ship then you also need me to sail her. You've killed the Second Officer and crippled the Captain, and that means that you have to keep me alive. And if you keep me alive long enough then eventually I'm going to kill you."

I had said too much and Thang didn't bother to answer me. He just lashed out with the barrel of his combat rifle and struck me squarely across the side of the face. I went down feeling as though my head had exploded and landed on my knees struggling to remain conscious. The stars did an erratic jig before my eyes and I had to close them for a moment. My mouth filled slowly with blood and I spat it out with a couple of dislodged teeth.

A hand helped me to rise, and dimly I recognized the hand of the old monk. He was saying something to Thang but it was in Vietnamese and I could only sense his tone of disapproval. Thang answered harshly, while his man on the bridge and the ex-winch operator who had brought Ching forward stayed impassive but with their rifles levelled warily.

I realized that I had almost made the same mistake that I had prevented Ching from making: the mistake of getting mad and getting myself killed to no purpose. It was both dangerous and pointless to act without thinking, or to antagonize Thang with mere words. For the moment the guerillas held all the cards and I had to ride easy until the situation changed in my favour; or at least until I knew the exact odds and at least something of what it was all about.

I stood straight and pushed the old monk away, swallowing some more of my own blood rather than spit again and let them see how badly I had been hurt. My head was still ringing.

Huynh Quoc became unhappily silent when I rejected his help, although it was obvious that he had been making little headway with whatever impression he had tried to make upon Thang. The guerrilla Section Leader made his own laws and obeyed only his own instincts. He watched me like a stoat with narrowed eyes, his whole stance completely alien to his simple yellow robe. The others waited for my next move.

I looked towards the scene of the fire and saw that the red glow had faded and that the flames were gone. There was nothing but clouds of smoke and steam shrouding the charred remains of the walls that had once enclosed the radio room. A dark grey pall was rising up to blot out the night sky, and mercifully there was no wind. The two seamen were still playing the jet from the hose over the jagged edges of the boards that ended in the black hole in the deck, but Ching had left them and was approaching the bridge. Ho Wan was beside him, and I noticed that the Bo'sun rated his own private guard with an alert rifle.

"The fire is out, sir," Ching reported.

"No more danger," Wan added briefly.

They stood waiting and I knew from their faces that they had both witnessed the blow that Thang had just struck. I wondered then what they were thinking. When the Japanese invasion forces had swept over Asia during World War Two a great number of the local people had been delighted to see their ex colonial masters, the big strong occidentals, kicked around. It had broken the myth of the white man's supremacy. Were Ching and Wan thinking something similar now?

I looked at the caked blood on the Bosun's face, matting one side of his proud mandarin moustaches, and at the iron restraint in his dark, measuring eyes. I looked at Ching's tightened lips and his fists clenched stiffly at his sides. And I knew that for a fleeting moment I had wronged both these men. James Ching and Ho Wan were one hundred per cent loyal, and even now they only needed my leadership to make a suicidal assault upon Thang and his thugs. I had to be sure that I only led them at the right time. I must not let them throw away their lives with no hope of victory.

"Thank you, Mister Ching," I said quietly. "Now take command of the bridge please. Get the ship under way and hold her steady on her course. Bo'sun, I want a couple of men with a stretcher to carry the Captain to his cabin."

"Aye, aye, sir."

They spoke with one voice. Ching started for the bridge and Ho Wan turned on his heel. Thang stopped them by saying harshly:

"Wait. I am in command here. I give the orders."

"The ship has to get under way," I told him bluntly. "We can't just drift on the open sea. And the Captain has to be carried to his cabin. What orders do you have to add?"

"I give all the orders," Thang snapped angrily. "You will not ignore me!"

We glared at each other, eyeball to eyeball, unblinking, and then Butcher spoke painfully from the deck between us.

"I'm still the Captain of this ship. I'm the man who gives the orders."

It was an unexpected interruption and Thang and I broke off our interlocked stares to look downward. Butcher lay on his back like some gross species of harpooned whale, but pain had sobered him and now his

51

eyes were open. They were grey eyes, the colour of the sea on a cold dawn.

I knelt beside him and said:

"I'm sorry, sir. I thought that you had fainted. What are your orders?"

He moved his head back to check that the fire was out, and then looked up into the arrogant eyes of Thang. Finally he looked back to me.

"The Second Officer?"

"Dead," I said quietly. "And the radio operator."

A new pain masked his eyes for a moment, and then he said:

"Carry on, Johnny—as you think fit. At least until we know what they want."

I nodded and his eyes closed.

I straightened up slowly. Ching was waiting for me with one hand on the companionway rail.

"The bridge, Mister Ching," I repeated. "Slow ahead and tell the helmsman to hold his course."

"The ship will change course," Thang said harshly. "You will go to the bridge and order the new course."

"Later," I said. "First I want to see the Captain comfortable in his cabin. And I want the Chief Engineer brought up to examine his leg."

"Course change first!"

"The Captain first!"

Thang lifted his rifle. Ching paused and half turned. The Bo'sun took a warning step forward and the remaining combat rifles bristled again.

"Let's get one thing straight," I told Section Leader Thang. "If you want the co-operation of myself and my officers in running this ship—and remember that you can't run this ship without our help—then you have to start acting like a human being. Captain Butcher needs a doctor. The *Shantung* doesn't carry a doctor but our Chief Engineer knows enough about the job to handle our routine first aid. I intend to see Jean Pierre fix a set of splints on that broken leg before I issue orders for any change of course."

I think Thang would have refused me, but the old monk intervened.

52

"Please, Mister Steele," Huynh Quoc said earnestly, "go to the bridge and do as Section Leader Thang asks. I will see that the Chief Engineer is brought up to attend your Captain."

It was a matter of face before my Chinese officers, and I knew that in the East face was important. Also I had to set a precedent for all my future dealings with Thang.

"Bring the Chief Engineer up first."

"I will do it," Lin Chi said abruptly.

She started up the companionway to the bridge. Ching blocked her way but I nodded to him to continue his ascent and he went up ahead of her. Thang merely tightened his lips with surpressed anger.

I heard Lin Chi use the voice pipe to the engine room. She spoke in Vietnamese and after a moment came back to the rail to look down at us.

"The Chief Engineer is being brought up," she said.

There was a strained silence, and then I heard Ching say loudly and clearly:

"Slow ahead engines. Helmsman, hold your course."

The engine room telegraph rang and I allowed myself a faint smile. Ching had not forgotten my last orders and had asserted himself sufficiently to carry them out. It was a face win for Ching as well as for myself.

I turned to look at Ho Wan. At the corner of the Bo'sun's mouth there was a slight crack across the caked blood, which indicated that he too had permitted himself a brief flicker of approval. With men such as these there was nothing lost that could not be regained.

"The stretcher, Wan," I said.

He nodded and turned away, carelessly ignoring his anxious guard. The seamen who had accompanied him to deal with the fire had been mustered on the deck behind us under the remaining armed Vietnamese, and he singled out two of them and sent them down to the saloon to collect the stretcher that was kept for emergencies in the cupboard behind the pantry. The two men went nervously with one of the guerillas following.

The strained silence was resumed. Thang was furious that the old monk and Lin Chi had usurped a little of

53

his authority, and I avoided his eyes rather than provoke him. Ho Wan folded his arms across his breast and waited calmly. The *Shantung* suddenly shuddered, like a drowsy creature emerging from a sleep, and then began to creep forward. Jean Pierre's Second Engineer had answered Ching's signal for slow ahead.

Another thirty seconds passed and then two seamen and their guard re-appeared with the stretcher. They brought it to the foot of the bridge and Wan and I carefully lifted Butcher while they manoeuvred the stretcher beneath his bulk. Huynh Quoc became solicitous and helped us to steady the broken leg, and Butcher groaned and fainted as we lowered him down. The Captain was a heavy man but Wan handled him gently.

Jean Pierre came hurrying on to the deck as we straightened a blanket over Butcher's form. The little Frenchman was in oil-stained overalls with only his peaked cap and shoulder bars to distinguish him from any other inhabitant of his hot and noisy world. He stared for a moment at the scene of the fire and then turned towards us. There was another armed guard at his back.

"*Monsieur* Steele, what is happening?"

"We've been hijacked," I admitted. "What's been happening in the engine room?"

His face became a grimace. In moments of affection Butcher called him Old Frog and now his expression fitted the name aptly.

"We heard an explosion from the deck, and then the Second Officer rang down from the bridge and ordered stop engines. He said that there was a fire. I stopped the engines, but before I could do anything else this creature appeared on the catwalks with two others." He indicated his armed shadow with a bitter gesture. "They told us to be still and await new orders from the bridge. They would explain nothing, but they pointed rifles at us and there was nothing that we could do. On the catwalks they were out of our reach."

He stopped as he saw the stretcher.

"Captain Butcher has a broken leg," I informed him. "That's why I wanted you up here."

54

The little Frenchman knelt and quickly pulled away the blanket. Butcher was still unconscious and Jean Pierre became anxious. With both hands he felt gently around the Captain's left leg.

"A bad break," he determined. "I can feel the bone."

"Can you fix it?"

He looked up at me and bit his lower lip.

"I can try, Johnny. I can perhaps set the bone in splints and give him a shot to kill the pain—but he needs a hospital, and a real doctor."

"At the moment I don't think there's any hope of getting either. You'll have to do your best, Jean Pierre."

He replaced the blanket and stood up.

"Were there any other casualties?"

"Two dead," I said quietly. "Ralph and David Kee."

His face tightened and he stared at me intensely from beneath the peak of his cap. Then he turned his gaze on Thang, and his voice trembled as he took a step forward.

"And you are responsible!" he accused.

I gripped his arm firmly.

"Easy, Jean Pierre. The battle's over. For the moment there's no point in taking any more casualties."

He looked at me and then at the Bo'sun, taking note of our bloodied faces, and then he accepted that the battle had been fought and lost. I motioned to the two men with the stretcher.

"Get the Captain to his cabin."

"No!" Thang had decided to assert himself again. "Take the Captain to the saloon. All the passengers will be taken there. It will be easier to keep all of you under guard in one place."

I hesitated, but I didn't have to make an issue out of it.

"The saloon will be better," Jean Pierre said. "We can lay him on the saloon table and there will be room to work."

I kept my face straight, for Jean Pierre had unwittingly robbed Thang of what would have been a little victory in the face game.

"Very well," I agreed. "Take him to the saloon.

Wan, you go with them. Jean Pierre will fix your face. After that come back here and get some of this mess cleared up. And check that starboard lifeboat, the one that caught fire. I want to be sure that she's seaworthy."

The Bo'sun hesitated, a flicker of interrogation in his dark eyes. Then it was gone so swiftly that Thang missed it. Ho Wan knew as well as I did that it was the port lifeboat that had been licked by the fire, and he also knew full well that I would never confuse port with starboard. He nodded blandly and I knew that he understood.

"Aye, aye, sir!"

Thang glared at me, his exasperation exploding.

"Enough! Now you go to the bridge and change the course!"

I fenced the positive command with nonchalant agreement.

"Of course, that was our bargain, wasn't it?"

I turned smartly and ascended the bridge. I didn't look back but I knew that Wan had taken the initiative and gestured the stretcher bearers to start moving. The small group started to walk away with their guards while Thang came up the companionway behind me.

Lin Chi stood back to let me pass, her face was still pale and she refused to look into my eyes. Ralph Yorke lay spreadeagled on his back just behind her with three bullet holes in his chest, and the yellow-robed monk whom I killed in turn was sprawled a few yards away. Ching was standing by the helmsman looking tense and uncertain, and a second seaman stood nervously by the telegraph. The Vietnamese guard with his combat rifle stood well back so that he could threaten them all.

Thang's rifle prodded me between the shoulder blades.

"Go into the chartroom."

I turned into the chartroom and waited. Thang came in and moved round to cover me without getting too close. He spoke to Lin Chi and reluctantly she came to join us. Thang was too smart to bow heads with me over the chartroom table. He left that to his fair sex fifth column while he stood back with the levelled rifle.

The navigation chart for the South China Seas was spread out upon the table. Lin Chi moved her fingers over it uncertainly for a moment and then brought it to rest on a spot just off the Vietnam coast south of the Mekong delta.

"Do you know this island, Johnny? It is called Hon Lai island."

I moved closer. The chart showed Hon Lai as a microscopic dot, uninhabited and unimportant, just a fly speck of land in the ocean.

"No," I said. "Why should I?"

"Because that is where we want to go. You must order the change of course."

"And if I refuse?"

"I will kill you," Thang promised. "My patience is finished, and if you will not co-operate at all then you are of no use to me."

I looked into his slitted eyes and knew that he meant every word. Lin Chi gently touched my bare arm.

"Please, Johnny, I do not want to see any more killing. We do not want to hurt any of you. It is not necessary if you do not try to fight us. Please do as we ask!"

I pushed her hand away and refused to look at her. I could not trust myself to speak. Instead I picked up the callipers and the slide rule that lay beside the chart and slowly plotted out the new course. For the moment I had no practical alternative.

Thang and Lin Chi watched me work, the guerilla leader coldly and the girl with worried eyes. When I had finished I did not wait for Thang to press me any further, for I saw no point in building up his face at the expense of my own over an issue I knew I could not win. I straightened up and called out briefly:

"Mister Ching, set a new course, sixty degrees northwest by north. We are sailing to a place called Hon Lai island."

Ching nodded and looked to the seaman at the helm.

"Hard to starboard," he commanded.

The helmsman spun the wheel, passing the spokes deftly through his hands, and slowly the bows of the *Shantung* began to swing round under the glittering

57

stars. The ship kept turning west until she had made almost the full circle and we could see the pale white swath of our own wake behind us. Then Ching concluded:

"Steady on sixty degrees, northwest by north."

The helmsman steadied the wheel and the ship settled on to her new course. Ching became silent and motionless, and I could taste bile in the back of my throat again.

Thang gave a satisfied smile that was matched by his armed companion.

Their initial victory, whatever it implied, was sealed, and the *Shantung* was heading back towards embattled Vietnam.

CHAPTER SEVEN

LIN CHI remained silent beside the chart table, looking into my face and hoping for some sign of conciliation; but she still had the AK-47 she had taken from me hooked by its strap across one slim shoulder, and her hair was still loose where I had untied her pony tail in the moments of our love-making. They were two sour memories and I did not want to be reminded. I didn't want to talk to her.

I went out on to the bridge, and although Thang scowled because I didn't ask for his permission he made no attempt to stop me. I walked back to where Ralph lay and knelt down to straighten his out-flung limbs and place his cap over his face. His eyes were wide and dilated and it was all that I could do for him until I could order the Bo'sun to have him taken below and prepared for a decent burial. I wondered how I was going to tell his little Eurasian girl in Singapore. Then I wondered how I was going to break the news to the Kee family and all David's laughing brothers and sisters in the tenement block behind Kowloon. They were two jobs that I didn't want to face, but they were my job. Perhaps Ching would want to visit the Kees, in fact I was sure that he would, but I would have to go along and do my part.

If the *Shantung* ever returned to Hong Kong.

If we ever again saw Singapore.

The only place we seemed certain of seeing was a seabound dot on the map named Hon Lai, which at the moment meant nothing.

I was still kneeling when I heard the smack of canvas shoes on the companionway, and I stood up as the little man with the perpetual grin came on to the bridge. He chattered briskly to Thang in Vietnamese, and when the Section Leader answered curtly he bobbed his head with its coolie hat repeatedly in acknowledgement. He carried his combat rifle loosely in his hands.

I waited until they had finished their conversation, and then caught his eye as he turned to depart.

"We've met before."

"Yes, Number One," he was pleased that I had remembered. "I am called Dinh. I am the Assistant Section Leader of this guerilla unit—the Number two man. This morning I was a winch operator."

"That's when the bomb was planted in the radio room, while you were mishandling the winch?"

Dinh nodded happily.

"It was a good diversion."

"And afterwards I suppose you just concealed yourself aboard the ship instead of returning to the shore?"

He gave another nod and another grin.

"That is so, myself and some friends who were also pretending to be dock workers."

"How many friends?"

Thang started forward but there was no need for him to intervene. Dinh was a smart little man too and he was giving nothing away. He just smiled more widely.

"Enough."

"And the guns?" I asked. "How did you get those aboard. The monks carried no baggage."

Thang spoke sharply in Vietnamese. There was no reason why I shouldn't know now, but just to be unpleasant he was refusing me any more answers. Dinh looked at me and shrugged his skinny shoulders, as though to him it didn't matter either way.

Then Lin Chi moved out of the chart room and said quietly:

"The rifles were in two of those crates marked apples which you watched being swung into the hold. When the time was ready Dinh and his comrades broke them open, and brought up the necessary arms to Thang and his monks."

Thang turned on her angrily. She had defied his

60

wishes, but whether it was because she felt that she owed me an explanation, or whether she was simply being defiant it was hard for me to tell. There was a conflict of command between them, but it was not to be resolved yet. There was a second interruption as Huynh Quoc climbed up to the bridge.

The old monk looked tired and flustered and his face was troubled. He had changed from the placid old man who had lectured us so calmly at the dinner table, and yet somewhere he fitted into all this and was part of it. He hesitated when he saw Thang and the girl arguing, but they became silent and Thang gave him an interrogative look.

"We have forgotten that two of your men are being held by the American girl," Huynh Quoc reminded him. "I think that it is time to effect their release."

Thang looked as though he had forgotten, he had been too busy insisting that I changed the course of the ship. He showed his teeth in an ugly smile and remarked:

"That is no great difficulty. We will do it now."

"Wait," the old man said. He turned to me and placed his hands together as though in prayer. "If you will go with us and take the gun from Miss Ryan then there will be no danger for anybody. If Thang and his men go alone then perhaps there will be shooting, and perhaps the American girl will be killed."

He was right, and even if I wanted to deny him I couldn't take that risk with Evelyn Ryan's life. It galled me to think that I who had given her the little automatic would have to be the one to take it away from her again, but again I had no choice.

"Mister Ching," I said. "You are in command of the bridge while I'm away. Don't take any risks with your own life. Do anything they ask that's within reason and which doesn't endanger the safety of the ship. If you have any doubts insist that I be brought back to the bridge."

Ching turned his head.

"Aye, aye, sir. I understand."

61

Thang tightened his lips and determined to have the last word.

"Dinh, you will remain here on guard. *You* are in charge of this ship."

Dinh nodded, and then looked at me and shrugged his shoulders and grinned. He was a jerky little man, like a puppet on a string, and he was beginning to irritate me again. However, the question of who was in command of the ship was hypothetical, I knew that I could trust Ching to stand by my orders.

Three of us descended from the bridge, Huynh Quoc, myself and then Thang. As we reached the boatdeck another armed guerilla came to meet us. The seamen who had helped Ho Wan to put out the fire had been removed, presumably to their quarters in the peak where they would be held under guard, and the guerilla had returned for fresh orders. Thang told him to fall in behind us, an extra rifle in case I gave trouble.

Lin Chi suddenly decided to come hurrying after us, perhaps she too was afraid that I might make trouble, and so we made a column of five as we continued to the passenger cabins. Even in bare feet I was a good eight inches taller than the rest of them, but I was out-gunned and out-numbered.

We stopped at cabin number four and Huynh Quoc opened the door and led the way inside. The first monk I had knocked unconscious was sitting on the edge of the bed, looking groggy and splashing his face with water from the hand basin. He looked scared when he saw Thang, shrinking back into his robe as though for a moment he had become a real monk, humble and retiring. Thang's lip curled and he cursed the man briefly, although a stronger reprimand was obviously in store once we had settled the issue in cabin two.

Lin Chi returned the man's rifle and he accepted it uncertainly. There was a dark bruise across his jaw and that gave me some satisfaction. He scowled at me and I scowled back.

Thang backed out of the cabin and motioned us on, but Lin Chi paused and gathered up my shirt and socks and shoes from the floor by the foot of her bed. She held them out to me with hope in her eyes.

"Please, Johnny."

She was trying to help me. The shirt had my gold rank bars on the shoulders and she was trying to restore some of my dignity before we went any further. It was a nice thought but in front of her companions it was just another degradation, a reminder of the fool that I had been, and I felt even more sour towards her. I took the shirt with ill grace and put it on, and then sat on the bed to replace my footwear. Lin Chi found my cap on the hook behind the door and returned it to me with the same hurt, hopeful expression. The severed halves of my necktie were still knotted to the hand basin tap so she could not return that.

Thang was getting impatient so I didn't dawdle. When I could see an advantage in getting him riled then I would do it, but there was no advantage at the moment. I didn't want him mad enough to blast Evelyn Ryan if she was slow to hand over her gun.

We went back into the passageway and turned the corner towards cabins three and two. The doors of both cabins were closed and Huynh Quoc halted before the second one and turned to face me. He put his hands together and his face was full of wrinkled concern.

"Please," was all he said. He and the girl seemed to be full of pleases, which was perhaps their way of making up for Thang and his company who never used the word.

I nodded my head and the old monk moved out of the way. There were now three rifles at my back as I knocked on the door.

"Who is it?" The voice was Janet Deakin's, calm and controlled.

"John Steele," I answered. "The Chief Officer."

There was a pause and then the door opened. Howard Deakin stood there, fully dressed now in grey trousers and a white shirt, and his face paled behind his spectacles when he saw that I was not alone.

"I'm sorry," I said lamely, and stepped into the cabin.

63

Janet Deakin was sitting on the bed, her hands resting in her lap and carefully cradling the little automatic that I had left with Evelyn Ryan. She had changed into her blue dress and seemed quite confident, although the gun was still alien to her personality. The two monks whom she held captive were sitting on the floor, shamefaced and surly but with their hands clasped on top of their cropped heads and showing her every respect.

The Deakins and the monks were alone. There was no sign of Evelyn Ryan.

The missionaries stared at me, and then at Thang and his armed companions who were right behind me. Two rifle muzzles pressed against my spine while Thang stepped forward and pointed his own rifle at the grey-haired old lady. Howard stepped automatically between them, unarmed and frightened but protecting his wife.

I moved quickly to ease him out of the way before Thang got rough, and fortunately Janet had the presence of mind to sit perfectly still.

"I'm sorry," I repeated. "But I lost the war. You'll have to give me back the gun."

She looked at me with shocked eyes, and I remembered that my face was swollen and thick with blood where Thang had knocked me down. The Bo'sun and I would probably make a good pair of matching bookends. A spasm of sadness passed over her face, and then she turned the gun in her hands so that she could hold it out to me butt first.

"I don't think that I could pull the trigger anyway," she said. "Although I pretend well. You learn how to look stern when you've been a school-mistress. That's what I was for a few years before Howard married me."

"Thank you," I said, and took the automatic from her hand.

I turned and threw it casually to Lin Chi. She stumbled back and caught it clumsily.

"It's yours," I reminded her. "Keep it in a safe place—if you have one."

Thang cursed his discomfited men and got them

scrambling to their feet, and then he rounded savagely on the Deakins.

"Where is the American girl?"

Howard set his face stubbornly. He didn't intend to help.

"She isn't here."

Thang glared at Huynh Quoc, and the old monk spread his hands and looked baffled.

"She was here when I released Lin Chi," was all that he could say. "They were all here together."

Thang snapped at the two ex-prisoners but got only a gabble of protest that evidently told him nothing. He swung back on the Deakins.

"The girl was here. Where did she go?"

"She didn't say."

I said quietly: "I think it will be best if you tell us anything you know. These people have taken over the ship and there are more than just the eight monks. We had some stowaways hiding in the hold. I don't know how many exactly but enough to swing all the odds in their favour. I've lost two of my officers dead already, and I wouldn't like to see Miss Ryan added to that list. These people are killers."

Howard hesitated and then said helplessly:

"I still don't know. She didn't say where she was going, or what she intended to do. She just said that she wanted to see what was happening."

I looked to Janet Deakin and her gray head inclined in agreement.

"That is true, Mister Steele. After you left us Evelyn began to feel a little uncomfortable in front of these men wearing just a see-through nightie. She gave the gun to Howard and we both went to her cabin and got dressed. We came back and waited for you to return. We heard more shooting which worried us very much. Then we felt the ship change course and Evelyn was sure that something was very wrong. She decided then that she would go and find out what was happening. She made these two Vietnamese gentlemen sit on the floor with their hands on their heads, and then she gave the little gun to me. Howard dislikes guns even more than I do. Evelyn went out and we haven't seen her since. That was ten minutes ago."

I knew instinctively that Janet Deakin wouldn't lie, not even for the benefit of someone like Thang. It would be against her nature, and the only way that she would ever conceal the truth would be with a stiff-lipped silence.

Thang believed her too. He started snapping orders and the two released monks and the armed guerilla who had accompanied us from the bridge departed in a hurry. I didn't speak their language, but I could guess at the nature of their orders. They would return to the bridge to pick up reinforcements and the rifles I had taken from the two monks, and then they would start to search the ship.

I could only console myself with the thought that at least Evelyn was no longer armed. She couldn't put up any serious resistance, and if I prayed perhaps she would come to no permanent harm. I cursed her for trying to play the female version of James Bond, or whatever the hell she thought she was doing.

CHAPTER EIGHT

TOGETHER with the Deakins I was marched at gunpoint to the saloon for safe-keeping. There the large dining table had already been cleared to accommodate the helpless form of the Captain. Jean Pierre had stripped off his greasy overalls and rolled up his shirtsleeves to his new task, while Hong hovered beside him with bowls of water and clean towels. Three guards stood at intervals around the room with raised rifles to watch them work.

Jean Pierre had cut away the cloth of Butcher's trouser leg to clear the broken limb, and I saw that the swab and the water in the bowl Hong held were both pink with blood. He looked up as we arrived and the Chevalier face had aged away, all his former jauntiness was gone.

"How is he?" I asked.

"Worse than I feared," he retorted grimly. "The bone is snapped into two pieces and has splintered badly. One piece had pushed through the flesh."

I moved closer and saw the ragged wound just below Butcher's knee. It looked ugly.

"I have given him an injection of morphine, and I have tried to set the bone. It is not a good fit," he concluded simply. He spread his hands in despair. "He needs a surgeon, Johnny, not an engineer who knows more about pistons than bones. Otherwise he will lose that leg."

Huynh Quoc was still with us. He came closer and asked humbly:

"I have some knowledge. Can I help please?"

Jean Pierre stared at him, and then at his guards.

"You're one of them?"

67

I nodded. "He has a little gun too. He's only shown it once but it's tucked away somewhere in the folds of that robe."

"Then I don't need his help," Jean Pierre decided.

Huynh Quoc closed his eyes for a moment, as though he had received a blow

Janet Deakin didn't offer, she just walked round the table and calmly took the bowl of hot water from Hong. The steward looked uncertain but she smiled at him.

"I've done this sort of thing before," she said.

Jean Pierre hesitated, the Captain was his Fat Friend and he was reluctant to trust that helpless bulk to a stranger with unskilled hands.

"I really have done it before," Janet Deakin assured him. "Our mission was a crude hospital for the local Vietnamese."

Jean Pierre relaxed his face, not a smile but a gracious gesture.

"Merci, Madame."

They bent together over Butcher's leg while Hong continued to hover anxiously. The wooden splints that were part of our basic medical kit were laid out on the table ready, and Hong straightened the straps with great care and moved them closer to the patient.

I turned to Thang, and because I wanted answers and not a clash of wills I tried to keep my voice calm.

"You heard our Chief Engineer—the Captain needs a hospital and a surgeon. How long will it be before we can expect to reach a port?"

Thang remained blank and I looked to Lin Chi. She hesitated and it was Huynh Quoc who gave me an answer.

"If all goes well, perhaps in two or three days."

"What about this island, Hon Lai—are there any medical facilities there?"

He shook his head. "No, I am sorry, there will be nothing at Hon Lai."

"Then why are we going there?" I came to the sixty-four-thousand-dollar question. "Why do you want the *Shantung*?"

"No more questions," Thang cut in sharply. "We

68

have a purpose for your ship, Chief Officer, but it is not necessary for you to know that purpose yet."

I turned back to him, angry because I believed that the old monk would have continued to give me answers.

"But why pick on the *Shantung?*" I asked. "What could you possibly want with a rusty old tub like this?"

"Your ship will serve our purpose," Thang said. "It was more easy to board and capture this ship than it would have been to take a ship with tight discipline. And this ship will not be so quickly missed when she fails to arrive in Singapore on schedule. A ship like this is often late in sailing or in reaching her destination." He scowled and added: "We did not expect so much trouble from you."

I bit off a smart answer on the tip of my tongue. Smart answers were no way out of this situation.

Howard Deakin said suddenly: "Who are you anyway? Buddhism is supposed to be the gentle faith. Buddhists don't practise violence, and they don't interfere in worldly affairs. You're not monks!"

Thang showed his teeth, the nearest I had seen him come to a laugh.

"You are correct. We are not monks—we have merely borrowed the yellow robe."

"Then you're Viet Cong."

Thang did not like the term and his face became cold again.

"We are guerillas of the National Front For Liberation—but in my case you are correct, I am a Communist. In Vietnam we have a choice: to become part of a Communist Empire, or to become part of the American Empire, because Vietnam is where the two empires meet. Perhaps I should use the word Power-bloc instead of empire, because empire is a word that neither side likes to use, except when accusing the other. But it is no matter, the choice of words is not important. The Communist Empire is at least an Asian Empire, and I am an Asian, so I choose to be Communist."

Howard turned his head and fixed the old monk with a bitter look.

"So you're all Viet Cong—and at dinner you had the

hypocrisy to give me a lecture on comparative religion!"

Huynh Quoc flinched and lowered his gaze. For a moment he was silent and then he gathered his robe close as though it could protect him and raised his face to meet the eyes of his accuser.

"I am a priest of the *Sangha*," he said in a low voice. "I have passed my examinations to reach the third rank. I am entitled to wear my robe—it is all that I have."

"Then you have shamed your robe, and broken your vows!"

Howard uttered the words more in surprise than continued anger, and the old monk bowed his head once more and repeated in a voice that had dropped another octave:

"Yes. I have shamed my robe—and broken my vows."

"And helped to kill two of my officers," I added bitterly.

"No." He looked up in anguish. "That was not meant to happen!"

"But two men are dead. Three men if you count one of your pseudo-monks."

"It was not meant to happen!" he cried again.

"Did you really expect to take over this ship without any kind of a fight?"

I was shouting back at him and Howard tentatively reached out a hand to restrain me. I realized then what the missionary had already understood. The answer to my question was yes. The old monk really had expected to take over the *Shantung* without a fight.

"Why?" Howard asked him quietly. "Why did you become involved?"

It was Lin Chi who answered for him. She stepped forward and said:

"Because only a real priest could arrange for eight monks to attend the Buddhist convention in Singapore. Only a real priest could succeed in getting them clearance from the South Vietnamese authorities, and in booking their passage. At the last moment seven of the monks were replaced by Section Leader Thang and six

70

members of his guerilla unit, but it was necessary for Huynh Quoc to accompany them and see them through the emigration formalities. It would not have been possible for the whole of the guerilla unit to have become stowaways. We had to get half of them aboard in this way."

"But why become involved at all?" Howard insisted.

"He became involved because of me," Lin Chi said quietly. "Huynh Quoc is a close friend of my father, and he is also my spiritual adviser. And also he is doing this for others, and because the task must be done. This is our plan—Huynh Quoc's plan—and we could not stay uninvolved in the final stages. We have to see it through."

"Enough." It was Thang's favourite conversation-stopping word, and he was making it plain that no matter who had done the planning he considered himself in effective command.

"You won't succeed with this," Howard warned him. "No matter what your purpose is you won't succeed. The American Air Force can catch up to this ship in no time, and I wouldn't mind betting that we are being scanned even now by the radar screens of one of our carriers or destroyers. Do you really think that they won't be suspicious when they notice that the ship has changed course? Do you really think that they won't send out planes to investigate?"

"Why should they?" Thang asked blandly. "This is an old ship. Even her Chief Officer calls her a rusty old tub. Such ships often turn back to port to make repairs, or because they have received a radio call to say that there is an unexpected consignment of cargo. Why should your American radar screens keep track of such an unpredictable ship."

"In this part of the world they just might check it out anyway."

Thang curled his lip. "I do not care. This is a British ship, with three American lives on board, and I do not think that the American Air Force would dare to sink us, even if they knew for certain that something is wrong. And what else could they do?"

71

Thang smiled when he received no answer and continued:

"Your wife and yourself, and the American girl when we find her, will make excellent hostages. That is why you were allowed to book passages on this ship. We could have found ways to deter you, but in fact we would have preferred even more American passengers to make hostages. Hostages are very useful things to have, and perhaps after this task is done we can find use for you again."

"No." Lin Chi said sharply. "After this task is done they must be released. The ship will be released. We have no right to hold them any further."

Thang turned upon her with sudden fury in his slitted eyes.

"We have every right! This is not one task but a tiny part of the whole war. The struggle does not stop until the people have won everywhere. Our victory will be just a small part, and we must go on to more and more victories. You are a selfish child if you cannot see beyond the one small battle that involves you personally."

Lin Chi answered him just as fiercely but in Vietnamese. They preferred to wrangle in their own language which none of us understood. The old monk tried to smooth things over and Howard and I left them to it and turned our attention back to the improvised operating table.

The job was finished and Butcher's leg was neatly bandaged and strapped in splints. Jean Pierre was making him more comfortable by placing a cushion behind his head and Janet Deakin was washing her hands. Hong was clearing away some of the bowls and towels.

"We've done our best," Janet said, "but *Monsieur* Lasalle is right, he does need a surgeon." She frowned at me and added: "You'd better let me attend to your face. It looks as though you've been doing about thirty rounds of bare knuckle fighting."

"It feels like it," I said wryly, and sat down.

I was still gritting my teeth and enduring when there came a sudden flurry of shouts and excitement from the upper decks. They were too muffled for me to distinguish what was happening and the raised voices were in Vietnamese anyway. Janet paused and I moved her hand and the red-stained towel away from my face. The argument between our captors had abruptly stopped.

Thang snapped something at his three guards, obviously an order to stay alert, and then he ran out with his rifle. Lin Chi and the old monk stood together and watched him go, as though wondering whether they should follow.

"What's happening?" I asked them.

Lin Chi looked at me and made a helpless gesture of her hands.

"I do not know."

We listened but the initial fuss was over, the shouting had stopped. At the same time there was an atmosphere of suspense around the ship, as though whatever was happening was taking place further away, beyond our hearing. Howard glanced at me.

"What do you think?"

"I don't know either," I admitted. "But I can make a guess."

"Evelyn?" he suggested, and looked worried.

That thought suddenly worried me too, although it wasn't my original guess. However, eventually we were both proved right.

We waited several minutes in helpless anticipation, and then we heard Thang returning. He threw open the door and half turned as he came inside. His face was furious and he kept his rifle levelled. Behind him, prodded along by three more rifles, was the calmly resigned figure of Ho Wan. The guerillas who followed the Bo'sun were the two pseudo-monks and the coolie guerilla who had been sent in search of Evelyn Ryan. Their search was over for the American girl was cradled limply in Wan's supporting arms, her chestnut brown hair trailing towards the deck.

"It is all right," Wan said as he saw our faces. "Lady is only unconscious."

Janet Deakin stared at his still undoctored face,

73

where the dried gore had begun to flake away. Then she looked at me and said in despair:

"Your bare-knuckles opponent, I suppose?"

"Not exactly," I said, "we're on the same side." And then to Wan. "What happened?"

"Your man tried to escape," Thang said angrily. "That was a very foolish thing to do. I am in a good mind to have him killed as a lesson to you all."

"He's the ship's Bo'sun," I said. "And I need him. If you kill or cripple any more of my officers you'll have to sail this damned ship yourself."

Thang fumed and shut up, and I asked Wan again: "What happened?"

Evelyn Ryan began to stir and before answering Wan set her feet gently on the deck. She opened her eyes and looked at him, and then she looked to me. She had heard my question.

"This stupid great reincarnation of Ghengis Khan slugged me," she said. "Not to mention scaring me half silly." There was a dark bruise above her right eye and she touched it gingerly. "If I didn't know how to ride a punch he would have knocked my head off. Instead he just knocked me cold."

"I not recognize passenger lady," Wan said apologetically. "I thought she was Viet Cong."

In the dark that would not be too difficult a mistake to make, for she was now wearing a pair of dark jeans and a dark shirt, a very practical rig-out for prowling by night. I looked at Wan for the third time and said:

"Start at the beginning."

"Aye, aye, sir." His face became bland to appease Thang, and so I guessed that Thang didn't know the full story either.

"When I leave the saloon I remind my guard that I have to clear the deck and see that the fire is okay. He has heard your orders so we go back to the boatdeck. We go to the place where the radio room has burned. I go close to the hole that has burnt through the deck. Then I jump down through the hole."

I smiled, for a moment I could picture the consternation of the guard when his prisoner had suddenly dropped out of sight to the deck below. Once, in a howling gale, I had witnessed the Bo'sun dive the full width of the *Shantung's* corkscrewing deck in two seconds flat to grab the collar of a man in danger of being swept overboard. I knew how fast Wan could move, but to a stranger it would come as a complete surprise.

Thang was looking furious again, so I wiped the smile off my face. Ho Wan continued just as blandly:

"I hear Viet Cong shouting on boatdeck, but I run through passageway between officers' cabins to starboard side. Then I climb up outside rail to boatdeck again. No Viet Cong on this side, all on port side. I go quickly to number two life-boat. Then I see the tarpaulin is open. I hear somebody inside the boat. Somebody jump out and attack me. I hit with fist."

He looked apologetic again. Evelyn moved away from him and straightened her hair with her hands. She said tartly:

"And I thought *he* was a Viet Cong—he looks villainous enough.'

"So would you if someone slammed your face open with a rifle barrel," I told her sharply. Then I looked to Wan again because I knew there was more.

"The real Viet Cong came," he said. "They hear the noise. But it was no good. The lifeboat radio was smashed too. Somebody smash that radio pretty good."

I turned to stare at Evelyn Ryan.

"Did you smash that radio?"

"Damn you, no!" she flared up at the suggestion. "I was trying to get a message out too. I saw that the radio room was burned out, and that you had lost control of the ship. I guessed that one of the lifeboats must have a radio, but Ghengis here came along just as I found the right one. The radio was already busted into little pieces."

"The next time you have a bright idea you might at least inform me." I was trying to keep my anger bottled up but some of it came out as sarcasm. "If you get in the way of my officers you might get killed. And just for the record the Bo'sun would have been more use to me if he had stayed free, and without your help he might have stayed free. He knows the inside of this ship better than you know the inside of your own handbag."

She glared at me and I wondered if I would ever see anything other than contempt and *I hate you* written in those honey-brown eyes. But this wasn't a game, it was for real, and she had just trumped what might have been my only ace.

Also I had to square up to the fact that our last possible radio link was gone. There was no more hope of communication with the outside world, and no hope of receiving any outside aid. In that moment it didn't occur to me to wonder where a nice, apple-pie-and-cookie-nourished little home-town girl like Evelyn Ryan had learned to ride out a punch. All I could see then was that the *Shantung* was isolated on the high seas, and that we who were aboard would have to solve our own problems.

CHAPTER NINE

IT was dawn when we first sighted the island of Hon Lai. It appeared as a watery green smudge on the horizon of the pale grey sea, and high in the brightening sky above the port bow the last faint star was fading into invisible space. Behind the ship our wake led back to the flush of morning red that soon gave birth to the rising sun.

Observing the daily glory of the sunrise was the main pleasure and compensation of the morning watch, but this was one occasion when I did not walk out on to the wing of the bridge and turn my head to act witness. Instead I watched the green island take shape and wondered what lay in store for us there. The chart could tell me nothing, except that the island was located some ten miles from the Vietnamese coast, which still lay over the horizon, and that as far as was known it was simply an off-shore dot of jungle and swamp covering less than a square mile. Our new masters were even less informative than the chart.

I had relieved Ching as we approached our destination, and he had been marched down to the saloon to take his rest under guard. He had looked weary after standing long hours on the bridge, almost a double duty watch, and I was feeling somewhat weary too. Neither of us had had any sleep. Also the side of my face was now beginning to throb and ache under the dressing where Janet Deakin had sewed three stitches to close up the skin above my cheekbone. Ho Wan had stolidly sat in the same chair after me and suffered five stitches in almost the same place.

A few feet behind me stood Thang, still wearing the

yellow robe and still holding his combat rifle. Two more of the armed pseudo-monks were positioned one on each wing of the bridge. None of the others were in sight but I had managed to compare figures with Wan before we had been parted and now we had a rough total of the odds against us. Four men had stormed the crew's quarters when the battle had started, and were now holding them prisoners in their own mess room, and Jean Pierre had reported that three men had invaded his engine room. There had also been two men on the bridge who were not monks when I first arrived on deck, and finally Dinh, the Assistant Section Leader. That made a total of ten stowaway guerillas, plus Thang and his five surviving monks. A total of sixteen hardcore Viet Cong, plus Lin Chi and her spiritual adviser, both complete with .38 automatics.

I wondered how the hell ten men had stowed away aboard the *Shantung* without being noticed, but then I remembered that I had been suffering from that kingsize hangover, and Ralph had been sleeping one off. And most fortunate of all for the enemy viewpoint, the Bo'sun had been ashore. Ho Wan had not returned to the ship until an hour before we sailed, but by then the guerillas had been hidden too deep in the hold. Thang and his unit had been more lucky than they deserved.

Hon Lai was coming closer, and there was a double line of black dots on the sea leading out towards us. I lifted my binoculars and brought the first one into focus. It was a sampan with one small brown man aboard wearing a pair of shorts and a coolie hat. He stood up and waved his hand and laughed, as though the *Shantung* was expected. I moved my glasses and the remaining sampans leaped into my double circle of vision one by one. They all had just one crewman aboard, some of them blinking and awakening from sleep, and others hauling in their hand lines where they had been idly fishing while they waited.

"You must steer between the two lines of sampans." Thang informed me calmly. "They mark a channel which is deep enough to allow the safe passage of the ship."

78

"Very ingenious," I said.

Thang shrugged. "We are well organized. We do not have the proper buoys, and in any case we did not wish to mark a permanent channel. The sampans were the simple answer."

I didn't intend to compliment him any more, and I turned to issue orders to the helmsman and the seaman by the telegraph.

"Engines half speed. Helmsman, turn the course three degrees to starboard."

Both orders were obeyed. The Telegraph jangled, and the helmsman turned three spokes of the wheel. The *Shantung* gradually lost speed as her bows turned to aim between the two rows of sampans. I moved back to the voice pipe to the engine room and blew down it to attract attention. Jean Pierre answered.

"Stand by." I said. "We're approaching within half a mile of the island. I might have to signal a rapid reverse engines."

"*Trés bien Monsieur Steele*, we shall be ready."

"The channel is deep enough," Thang repeated. "We are not fools. We do not want this ship grounded any more than you do."

"All right, how far do I take her into the channel?"

"All the way. It will lead you into the narrow cove. There the water is also deep enough to float your ship. You will stop engines there and lower the anchor."

I walked forward and watched as we neared the first two sampans.

"Helmsman, one more degree to starboard."

I didn't look round but I felt the ship obey. The bows veered round just a little more and we were heading directly down the wide lane between the two rows of moored crafts, all of them had a rope with a stone weight thrown overboard to hold them in place. As we passed between the first pair the boatmen stood up and waved their coolie hats and cheered. The welcome was repeated all along the line.

"Slow ahead engines."

The telegraph jangled again and the response was prompt. The ship lost more way and proceeded slowly.

"I shall need my Bo'sun on deck," I said. "And enough of the crew to man the anchor windlass."

Thang was suspicious. "I do not trust your Bo'sun. He is a troublemaker. The two of you together can cause much trouble."

"I still need him on deck. Nobody else can handle his job."

There was a silent pause behind me and I guessed that Thang was scowling. Then he gave an order and the pseudo-monk on the port wing slung his combat rifle over one shoulder and hurried down the companionway to vanish into the forecastle.

I continued to watch the double row of sampans, and the island that was now dangerously close. Dense jungle and tall palm trees overhung the narrow, sand beaches, and slowly it seemed that the island itself was opening out to receive us as we approached the cove. The sampan boatmen were still laughing and shouting to one another, and the monk sentry on the starboard wing was waving back. Thang remained unexuberant, and from the corner of my eye I saw him glance anxiously skyward.

"Make the ship go faster," he said. "This is too slow."

I knew why he was worried. The sky was blue now and the sunrise was well advanced behind us. There was no cloud and the morning was bright and clear and a stray American aircraft flying anywhere in the vicinity would almost certainly spot what was happening. I couldn't imagine even the dullest pilot remaining uncurious about this scene, and neither could Thang.

"I thought you didn't want the *Shantung* grounded," I said. "You must be mad if you think I'm going to drive her in here at full speed."

Thang was frustrated. He knew that I was right, and at the same time he knew that I wouldn't mind at all if the whole American Air Force came to investigate. It was a chance he had to take.

Unfortunately I couldn't order the engines any slower than dead slow, and the blue skies were still empty as we crept cautiously between the last of the sampans and into the mouth of the cove. It was a long, narrow inlet, a stubby blue finger between green-crowded yellow beaches, and not quite double the width and length of the *Shantung*. It was a very tight fit.

Ho Wan appeared on deck, with three of our Chinese crew and two armed guards. He stared for a moment at the close walls of tangled foliage, and then glanced up at the bridge.

"Man the anchor, Bo'sun!"

"Aye, aye, sir."

He nodded and urged his men forward to the point of the bows. They took their places by the electric windlass while he leaned over the side to gauge the depth of the sea. The *Shantung* was now half-way into the cove."

"Stop engines!" I ordered.

The telegraph jangled, and the thud of the screw ceased altogether a moment later. The *Shantung* continued to drift slowly forward under her own momentum. In the trees a number of birds shrieked and called attention to our arrival.

We were well into the cove and nosing up to the far shore when the Bo'sun abruptly raised his hand.

"Engines full astern!"

Jean Pierre was quick to answer me in the engine room and the single screw began to churn in reverse. The *Shantung*'s forward movement was halted and she gave a shudder before beginning to edge back.

"Stop engines!"

I looked at Thang. "Does this satisfy you?"

"This is excellent, Chief Officer." He showed me his teeth. "You have behaved very sensibly."

I turned away again. I didn't want compliments from him either.

"Bo'sun, drop the anchor!"

"Aye, aye, sir!"

The windlass motor started and the chain rattled noisily out of its locker, causing more consternation among the startled birds. The anchor splashed into the cove and sank.

"Finished with engines," I said reluctantly.

The telegraph jangled for the last time, the engines

stopped and the ship became still. I walked away from the helm and out on to the wing of the bridge, and looking back I watched the fleet of sampans entering the cove behind us and converging upon the helpless *Shantung* like a flock of sea-borne vultures.

The next half hour provided a remarkable display of speed, improvisation and efficiency. The sampans were quickly sculled ashore where more bustling little Vietnamese in black pyjamas and coolie hats appeared from the jungle, dragging behind them large sections of camouflage netting. The nets were loaded on to the sampans and rapidly ferried out to the *Shantung*. The Viet Cong then swarmed aboard, as active as monkeys and as busy as beavers, and effectively draped the netting all over the ship. More sampans put out from the shore laden with fresh cut branches which soon flourished everywhere, until eventually the whole ship became a shouded island of green leaves and netting in the middle of the cove. From the air she would be invisible to the naked eye, and only an electronic camera would be able to distinguish her from the rest of Hon Lai.

Thang had disappeared to take charge of the cover-up operation, and so I remained quietly on the bridge with the pseudo-monk guard. The Bo'sun and his sailors had been returned to the peak, but I endeavored to stay unnoticed in the background to avoid being ordered below. I wanted to watch what was happening.

There must have been at least two hundred armed men engaged in the overall task, and when the camouflage job was done they were far from finished. They slowed down a little and relaxed, because now they could work under cover, and I watched with new amazement as a large raft made up of cut logs was poled out from the far end of the inlet. It was a clumsy craft but it did not have far to travel, and the men on board lifted up the trailing nets to bring it underneath and close against our hull.

Before the raft moved under our bows and out of my sight I had identified its cargo as a twenty-five pounder field gun.

I moved forward to observe as the little man with the skinny frame and the maddening grin unslung his AK–47 and took his place behind the electric winch. Assistant Section Leader Dinh then proved himself to be far more competent than when he had been loading our routine cargo in Saigon. He took charge of the deck in addition to operating the winch, and in a very professional manner he hoisted the artillery piece aboard. There was a brief delay while some of the obstructing nets were temporarily cleared back, and then he swung the derrick arm forward and lowered the field gun gently in the bows.

A group of five men quickly released the ropes and wheeled the heavy gun away. The winch rattled as Dinh brought back the derrick arm, and the camouflage netting was quickly replaced to form a broken canopy over the bows. Through it I saw that the empty raft was being poled back to the shore.

I looked below again. The five Viet Cong were obviously a trained gun team and were deftly manoeuvring their nearly two-ton piece of heavy fire-power into a war-like position, pointing threateningly forward. I knew that that baby could fire both high-explosive and armour-piercing shells, and I watched as they set it up and then used a large number of heavy ropes to secure it firmly to the foredeck.

By the time the job was done the raft was returning with a second twenty-five pounder balanced amidships. That too was hoisted aboard as professionally as the first, and a second gun team wheeled it into a supporting position.

The *Shantung* was being crudely converted into a makeshift warship, and to add the final touches the sampans sculled out again with two Chinese-made, 7.92 millimeter machine guns that were manhandled up to the bridge.

Thang came to supervise the installation of the machine guns and he seemed surprised to find me still there.

"You should be below!" he snapped.

83

"You've had a busy morning," I said. "You must have forgotten to give the order."

"Then you must go below now!"

I shrugged. "Okay, but what's it all about? Are you hoping to start up your own Viet Cong Navy? Because if so you won't last five minutes against the first real gunboat you meet."

"Enough, No questions. You go below."

He wasn't in a genuine bad mood because everything was going too smoothly his way. He merely talked like a snapping clam out of habit. However, I didn't expect to learn any more and there was no point at all in resisting with a whole army of his friends aboard. I allowed myself to be marched below.

The saloon was comparatively quiet and peaceful. The Captain was still laid out on the dining table with Jean Pierre sitting close beside him. The Deakins sat together looking tired and subdued. Ching was fast asleep in a chair and I knew that Ho Wan would be kept locked in the peak with the crew. There were three of the original yellowrobed guards in attendance, leaning casually against the bulkheads, but of the old monk and Lin Chi there was no sign. I presumed that they were resting in their cabins. There was only one absentee who should have been present.

"Where is Miss Ryan?" I asked.

It was Janet Deakin who answered me:

"She went to her cabin. She had a very bad headache where your Bo'sun knocked her down, and she was feeling ill. I managed to persuade mister Huynh Quoc that she could do no harm now that there are so many of his Viet Cong allies on board, and so he allowed her to go."

I was relieved and disappointed: relieved that she wasn't doing anything foolish, and disappointed that she wasn't there. I felt that I owed her at least a couple of apologies. That girl had courage and last night I had failed to appreciate it.

I turned to Butcher and saw that despite the pain and stubble on his face he was at least conscious.

"Good morning, sir," I said quietly. "How are you feeling?"

"In need of a drink," he said bluntly. "But Old Frog says I shouldn't have one. I think he's afraid that the stocks might run low and he'll have to go on short rations himself."

Jean Pierre smiled. "That is right. For you, only orange juice and coffee."

Butcher made a grimace, and then he became serious and his eyes steadied on mine.

"What's happening, Johnny? What are they doing to my ship?"

I took off my cap and sat down at the table, and then I told him all that I knew. When I had finished he was silent for a moment and then he rolled his head to look at me.

"You never did learn how to play chess, did you, Johnny?" He waited until I shook my head and then continued: "Well, there's one rule that you have to learn right now. The game is never over until the last move is played. Remember that. This fellow Thang is on top now and it looks as though he must have a winning game. But a game like that can make the other fellow over-confident, and then he's liable to make mistakes." He smiled briefly. "That's the only way I ever beat Old Frog, when he gets over-confident and makes mistakes."

"On the contrary," Jean Pierre said, "it is the only way in which I can beat you."

Butcher raised a limp, deprecatory hand. "At least he agrees with me. The point is, Johnny—even if you can't make a positive move you still have to keep up the pressure, and have your key pieces in position to exploit any of Thang's mistakes."

"I think I understand all that," I said. "But at the moment I do have one positive move in mind."

"What's that?"

I told them and they exchanged dubious glances.

"Be careful," Butcher said. "I've already lost two officers. I don't want to lose a third."

"They need me," I reminded him. "They have no

85

one else to sail the *Shantung*. With my own neck I can afford to take a few risks."

There was no more to discuss and so I called to Hong who was lurking in the pantry and ordered some breakfast. After a few minutes he brought out a tray with ham and eggs, toast and coffee, and while he served them I said softly:

"Hong, they're letting you move fairly freely, aren't they?"

He looked at me uncertainly.

"Yes, Mister Steele. Now that the ship has stopped they let me serve food for passengers and officers, and for themselves. Everybody have to eat."

"That's fine." I nudged him to continue pouring my coffee and went on: "If we manage to distract these guards for a few moments do you think you could sneak out and get to my cabin? I must be the last one for breakfast, and you won't be missed until the next meal."

He looked apologetic, and scared.

"I am not hero-man, Mister Steele."

"That's okay," I said. "I just want you to go to my cabin and hide in the shower cubicle till I arrive. That's all. I'll do the heroics."

His round face was worried, but finally he nodded. He served my fried eggs and for the first time in three years broke both yolks in the process. He looked flustered but I smiled and he hurried back to his pantry. He was no hero-man and he didn't understand, and he hadn't even asked why, but I felt confident that he would at least try to do as I asked.

I drank half my coffee and started to eat, and wondered how I could create a diversion. Then Jean Pierre smiled and winked one jaundiced eye.

"Don't wrinkle your brow, Johnny. You spoil that handsome face."

He stood up and set his cap at an angle as he crossed to the small bar where Hong kept the table wines and the after-dinner brandy. Casually he poured himself a cognac. The three guards had come alert and watched his movements with suspicious eyes.

"French cognac," Jean Pierre said. "Like everything French it is unsurpassable—like me." He sipped from the glass and smiled to include everybody. "Come my friends, why should we be miserable just because we are prisoners. Let us make the best of it and drink some of this excellent cognac."

He offered the bottle to the armed monks, but they merely stared back at him with narrowed eyes. Only one of them bothered to shake his head.

"Ah, well," Jean Pierre shrugged and looked at the Deakins. "Will you join me in an early morning cognac?"

"I'm sorry," Howard Deakin said stiffly. "We don't touch alcohol."

"Such a pity, how else can you drink, drink, and be merry?"

Jean Pierre shrugged again, and took another drink. Then he set the glass down, spread his hands in an eloquent gesture, and raised his eyebrows towards the ceiling. In a perfect imitation that only another Frenchman could make he began to sing:

> *"Thank heaven, for little girls,*
> *For little girls grow bigger every day . . ."*

It was his party piece, the charade he enjoyed most of all. I had watched his performance a hundred times before, usually in a shoreside bar when the hour was late, the smoke was thick, and the bar girls were laughing at his antics. Then he always wore the flat-topped straw hat that was part of his shore-going gear and his only prop. Now he made do with his official company cap and without his boozed and appreciative audience, and still the mimicry was well done.

> *"Thank heaven, for little girls,*
> *They grow up in the most delightful way . . ."*

He paused in front of Janet Deakin and removed his cap with a sweeping bow.

"Madame! Voulez-vous danser avec moi, si'l vous plait?"

Janet was startled, she stared at him and then at me, and I gave her a microscopic but sober nod. She realized then that our Chief Engineer had not taken an abrupt leave of his senses. She stood up and bravely accepted his invitation.

"With pleasure, *Monsieur!*"

They began to dance, carefully and politely, and then with less care and more grace as they realized that together they could pick out a waltz step with only Jean Pierre's voice to guide them. They made a strange couple, and yet for a moment the little grey-haired missionary's wife seemed to be enjoying herself. Howard watched them, while Ching had also woken up to stare. The three guards gazed at them with blank faces but baffled eyes, and slowly they relaxed.

Jean Pierre finished his song and brought Janet to a final halt where they had started beside her husband. He made a gallant bow and handed her back.

"*Merci, Madame!* And *merci* to you also, *Monsieur!*"

"*Merci, Monsieur.*" Janet made a curtsy.

"*Merci,*" Howard repeated, but looked as though he still didn't know why.

"Perhaps you are right," Jean Pierre said in answer to his expression. "It is too early to drink cognac and make merry. You must forgive an old Frenchman who cannot admit that he has grown old."

He smiled and then returned to the bar and picked up his half finished glass of cognac. He emptied it, and then shrugged his shoulders expressively towards the watching guards. Then he came calmly back to the table and sat down again as though nothing had happened.

I finished my ham and eggs and was careful not to look towards the pantry. I hoped that by now it was empty.

Twenty minutes later Huynh Quoc looked into the saloon. I had been waiting for one of our English-speaking captors to check that all was in order, and if I could have planned it the old monk would have been my personal choice. I tried not to smile at my luck as his yellow robe and the brown, wizened face appeared in the blurred frame of my half closed eyelids. I was slumped in a chair as though like Ching I was trying to sleep, and I groaned loudly and stretched as I pretended to wake. I opened my eyes fully and gave the old man a deliberately sour look.

"Is anything wrong?" he enquired.

"Yes," I said bluntly. "I've had a long night and I need some sleep—especially if you want me to take the *Shantung* out to sea again when you've finished all the little re-fitting jobs on deck. But I can't sleep sitting up in this damned chair. It's breaking my back! Is there any good reason why I can't go up to my cabin and turn into my bunk for a few hours?"

He put his palms together and contemplated. He was hesitant but he was still the weakest link, for there was genuine humanity in his soul. Now that he had more than enough men on call it was no longer necessary to keep us all confined together and he had already given way to Evelyn Ryan. Finally he looked up and gave way to me.

"Very well, Mister Steele. You can go to your cabin, and your Third Officer can also go to his cabin. But I will have to place armed guards outside both doors."

"That's fine," I said. "All I want is to sleep."

He nodded and went out to find two men whom he could post for extra guard duty. When he came back I woke Ching and we were both escorted back to our cabins. Ching was pleasantly surprised, and I reflected that perhaps he really would get some proper rest. I had unexpectedly achieved that much even if my other plans failed.

The old monk accompanied me and the armed guard to the door of my cabin and there he looked at me doubtfully for a moment.

"Please do not lock your door," he said. "Then the guard can quietly check that you are inside without disturbing you. I wish you a pleasant sleep."

"Thank you," I answered. "And goodnight."

I gave him my key as a sign of my good faith, and then went inside and closed the door on him. I leaned my back against it for a moment and listened. I heard him speak with the guard and then heard the shuffle as the guard took up his position, and then there was the faint sound of sandals and the trailing robe departing. I would have smiled but smiling hurt my face.

I crossed quietly to the shower cubicle and drew open the curtain, and the round, frightened face of Hong stared out into my own. He gave a little jump and then steadied again as he recognized me. He was standing to attention with his arms by his sides, with his steward's jacket buttoned up neatly as though he was awaiting a Captain's inspection. I put a warning finger to my lips just in case he hadn't worked it out that we could be overheard.

"You've just earned a promotion," I told him in a barely audible murmur. "For the next couple of hours you're going to be the Chief Officer."

I put my cap on his close-cropped head and his eyes were bewildered under the hard peak. Then I started to strip off my white shirt with the gold bars and he began to understand. His nerve-ends were as jumpy as a pack of fleas but he took off his own jacket and hurriedly donned the shirt in its place.

I steered him to my bunk and with some trepidation he lay down. I threw a sheet over him so that only his shoulders with the rank bars were visible and pulled the cap over his face.

"Pleasant dreams," I murmured. "When the guard looks in keep your face turned and pretend to be asleep."

Hong nodded dumbly, and I promised myself that when all this was over I would buy a big pile of presents for that young wife and the three little babies he had in Hong Kong.

I left him and moved over to the open port that looked out on to the boatdeck. I had to wait a couple of minutes until the deck was clear and then quickly I wriggled out. This was the most hare-brained part of my whole plan, but all that I could do was run like the blazes and hope that I could get clear without being spotted. Fortunately my cabin was too far back to be in full view of the bridge, and those sagging camouflage nets which were draped everywhere over the superstructure made a tangled maze of shadowy green curtains to screen me from view. I dived under the nearest lifeboat and lay flat in the scuppers and there was no outcry behind me.

I was sweating, but so far so good. I lifted my head and saw that the visible sections of the boatdeck were still clear. Then I turned my gaze outward to the continuing blanket of netting that hung down outside the hull almost to the sea level below. I jumped for the netting, caught it, and scrambled rapidly down as though I were descending the rigging on one of the real old-time sailing ships. I feared that the net would collapse and dump me into the sea with a heavy splash that would attract attention, but it merely sagged and swung me in so that my bare shoulders scraped some of the excess rust off the hull as I slithered down.

I reached the cool, welcoming embrace of the sea, released my grip on the net and began to swim slowly back towards the stern of the ship. I made no sound, and because most of the activity was taking place on the other side of the hull I was able to remain unseen.

I even began to believe that this was one move which I just might be able to play out to a successful conclusion.

CHAPTER TEN

I SWAM as far as the propeller and steadied myself for a moment against the shaft, hidden in the shadow of the giant triple blade that was only half submerged. Through the square pattern of the netting hanging down from the other side of the ship I could see a few of the sampans still plying a slow ferry service to the far shore, but most of them had now been withdrawn. I listened but I could hear no sounds of movement on the poop deck immediately above, and so I left my sanctuary and pushed forward again. I filled my lungs with air and then ducked my head and dived to get under the last curtain of net.

As I went down the salt water soaked through the dressing on the side of my face and stung along the stitched line of my cut cheek like burning acid. I almost floundered to the surface with the shock, but gritting my teeth I plunged deeper and swam on until my lungs were empty. I bobbed up for more air and a quick glimpse of the cove mouth and the open sea beyond, and then without wasting any time turning my head I dived again.

The water was clear and so even by swimming underwater I could still be seen from the *Shantung*'s deck, but there had been no signs of any activity at the stern and at least I could cover half the risks and stay invisible from the shore.

I turned while still under the surface and swam strongly for the opposite side of the cove, putting the ship between myself and the sampans. I had to come up once more to refill my lungs, but when they were near to bursting for the third time my hands struck the sand beach as it inclined upwards. I turned on my back and let my momentum ground me in the shallows, and as my nostrils emerged I breathed in more air. Some of the receding sea-water drained up my nose and caused me to cough and splutter.

I blinked the water out of my eyes and looked back to the ship. The old freighter was just a shrouded outline beneath the mass of camouflage, and now she seemed quiet and undisturbed. The heavy artillery had been installed in the bows and there was no longer any movement there, and again the bulk of the ship blocked me off from the view of the sampans.

There was no one looking in my direction from the ship's deck and so I took the last open risk in a mad scramble. The narrow strip of beach at this point was a bare ten yards wide and I lunged out of the sea and sprinted across in three tightly-shaved seconds, one for each stride before I threw myself headlong into the undergrowth at the foot of the palms.

I wriggled deeper into my new sanctuary of green, and then listened for any outcry from the ship or the far shore. There was none and so I risked raising my head again and looked back. The *Shantung* was still peaceful, and except that she was floating on the blue sea she might have been a lost temple of some long dead civilization, strangled by an enveloping forest of ropes and leaves.

I crawled further away from the beach until it was safe to stand up, and then breathed deeply for a few minutes to restore my energies. The birds worried me with their screeching, they seemed to consider this densely wooded island their own sanctuary, but as they had been crying and making protest ever since I had brought the *Shantung* into the cove I could hope that their present complaint would go unnoticed.

I didn't know how long Hong would be able to fool that guard outside my cabin door, and so I did not have too much time to waste in catching my breath. Now that I had succeeded in getting ashore unseen the next step was to work my way around the head of the inlet to reach the busy side of the cove. In respect for the birds, and any stray Viet Cong who might be in the area, I began to ease my way through the tangles of trees and foliage as silently and unobtrusively as possible.

The trees became higher and the undergrowth more difficult to penetrate as I moved further inland, but after ten minutes I judged that I was level with the far end of the cove. I turned to my right, moving warily, and soon the *Shantung* was again visible through a curtain of leaves and branches.

Some splashing sounds and a muffled voice made me crouch down and become alert, and after a few minutes of straining my eyes and ears to pierce the blurred tangle of greenery I realized what was happening. There was a sampan pulled into an inlet that drained into the cove, and two men in black pyjamas and coolie hats were carefully spreading cut branches over the deck and the central canopy. A little further away I heard the snick and rustle of more branches being cut down, and I guessed that the sampans which were no longer needed were all being drawn back from the cove and camouflaged.

I backed off and accepted that I had to make a wider sweep round the head of the cove.

It took me half an hour of careful weaving and ducking through the close trees, with frequent stops to untangle myself from the undergrowth, or merely to listen and ensure that I was not walking into any unwanted company. The jungle was all virginal and unmarked on this side, which helped to reinforce my conclusion that any base that the guerillas maintained must be on the opposite side of the cove.

When I started to circle again I soon encountered the inlet, just a shallow trickle here and too narrow to float a sampan, but still I paused for a long moment before I dared to cross. The clear water barely came up to my knees and I stepped gently on the pebbly bottom to avoid making any splashes that would betray me in turn. The jungle swallowed me up and I left the faint ripple of the stream behind.

I completed my circle and went into a crouch again as the *Shantung* re-appeared through the trees. The cove was quiet, the blue water unruffled, and there were no more sampans to be seen. I lowered myself on to my belly and began to snake my way forward. I was now on the starboard side of the ship, and on the opposite side of the cove from which I had started.

I came to a halt when I reached the edge of a narrow footpath. I could hear voices and see men in more of the wide coolie hats moving beneath the trees, and realized that here there was network of recently trodden paths that led away from the strip of beach where the sampans had been landing. I wriggled backwards until I was enveloped in foliage once more, and then made another wide circle, this time following the inland direction of the tracks.

After another ten minutes I was laying low on the edge of the nearest path again, and I could see where they were all leading. There was a small clearing and I could see the indentations of the broad rubber wheels where the two artillery pieces had once stood in the shadow of the trees. At the back end of the clearing a sloping tunnel ramp had been dug down to the entrance to an underground bunker, and one man with a combat rifle was standing in the doorway looking bored.

I guessed that the object of my quest had to be somewhere inside that underground bunker.

I started on the final circle that would bring me on to the roof of the bunker behind the guard, and now I could feel a definite sense of urgency. I was close and there wouldn't be much time. Right now the majority of the guerillas were busy with the task of concealing their sampans, but it was a job that would not take them long and then they would start returning to their base.

Behind the bunker there was more virgin jungle, tall ferns, long grass and bushes intertwined beneath the taller forest trees and the splayed crowns of the palms. Here my vision was limited by barriers of green to a few yards and I had to trust to my sense of direction. The need for haste was counter-balanced by the need for silence, and I approached as though I was stepping on eggs in a maze of fragile glass.

A branch rustled to my left and I froze. There was no

wind and no bird had taken wing, and yet something had moved. I stopped breathing and sank tentatively to one knee. Perhaps the Viet Cong were smart enough to have a guard lurking behind their bunker. If so I would have to deal with him before I dared to tackle the man in the tunnel doorway. I cursed because it was an unwanted complication and an extra risk, but I had come too far to turn back.

I eased myself towards the branch that had rustled. All the leaves were now still and I began to sweat. Perhaps he was aware of my presence too, and almost certainly he would be armed. And he couldn't be expected to know that I was the Chief Officer who had to be kept alive to sail their captured prize. I was no longer wearing my cap and rank bars.

I paused again. If that rustling branch had been caused by a man then he had moved. The jungle was silent. Even the birds were holding their breath. The green curtains were still. My heart pumped rapidly and my neck felt painfully stiff as I twisted my head to make a slow vision sweep all around me.

A leaf moved. There was a blur of black beyond it and I sprang with every ounce of power in my tensed leg muscles. The screen of leaves tore apart under my weight and I carried a slim but fighting human form violently to the earth. As we crashed down my left hand grasped for the throat and my right fist was already streaking for the jaw, and only just in time I saw the wide-staring honey-brown eyes and opened my hand to clamp it hard over her mouth.

My weight crushed her to the damp earth and she stopped squirming as she recognized my face. Her heart was racing even more frantically than mine and I could feel her whole body quivering. I drew my hand down from her freckled nose when I realized that she couldn't breathe, and then hesitantly removed it from her mouth altogether.

"Miss Ryan," I said in an ungracious whisper, "just what the hell do you think you're doing?"

She lay underneath me, too deflated to struggle, but with an effort she gave me a steady answer.

"I was looking for a radio. The Viet Cong seem to have blown up or smashed every set on the ship, so it seemed only fair to try and borrow one of theirs for a few moments. They must have a radio somewhere on this island in order to make contact with the mainland."

I relaxed and pushed myself away from her, and slowly she sat up and began to pick the leaves out of her chestnut hair. She was wearing her dark jeans, the blur of black that I had glimpsed through the branches, and her dark red shirt. Her clothes were still wet from her swim ashore. She gave me a cool look and had the brass nerve to throw my own question back at me.

"And for the record—just what the hell do you think you're doing?"

"Looking for a radio," I admitted. "We seem to make a habit of working on parallel lines." An hour ago I had been prepared to apologize to her but now she had me vexed again. "Isn't it time you stopped playing the Lone Ranger and gave me enough credit to think of the obvious. You fouled-up the Bo'sun when I sent him to check the lifeboat radio, and now you're getting in my way here!"

"Don't get shirty," she retorted. "You're not always around when I think of the obvious. You're usually busy on the bridge."

I had to bite my teeth together and remember that we were in no position to raise our voices and start a fight. She realized it too and became more suitably chastened.

"I am sorry, Mister Steele. I'm not deliberately trying to get in your way. I'm trying to help you find a way out of this mess."

With those freckles and that tone of voice it was impossible to stay mad with her. She looked too young and innocent.

"Okay," I said. "I'm sorry too—but what do I do with you now?"

At that she smiled. The college girl look vanished and the freckles didn't count, with that smile she was all woman.

"I guess you're lumbered with me," she said cheerfully. "We have to work together now."

I was reluctant. I would have preferred to send her back to the ship, but probably she wouldn't make it safely, and anyway I had the feeling that she wouldn't go.

"I was trying to reach that bunker," I said. "If they do have a radio then it must be inside. Can you stay behind me and keep quiet?"

"I was heading for the bunker too, and I've got this far!"

I nodded wryly to accede her point and then turned away. I started to move forward but she touched my arm.

"Watch out that you don't fall into another entrance," she warned. "These bunkers often form a complex of tunnels stretching underground for miles, and they have to have more than one way out."

I stared at her. "Do you think that this is some kind of a permanent base?"

She frowned. "I am not sure, but I think it's probably just a staging point they use for bringing in sea-borne supplies, rice and ammunition for the north. Today's operation is something special."

She looked into the upper branches of the trees and added:

"There are too many birds here, which means that normally there are not many people. In Vietnam all the birds are dead or departed, the war has seen to that, and most of them were smart enough to fly further away than this place."

I was curious. "How do you know so much about birds?"

She smiled. "I was born on a farm in Oklahoma. We had lots of birds there, and fields of yellow corn that grew as high as your shoulder." She looked nostalgic. "I often wish that I was back there."

She was being truthful, but at the same time she had evaded the question. She hadn't told me what I wanted to know. But perhaps that was because I didn't know what I wanted to know. I had the feeling that I hadn't asked the right question. However, time was being wasted and the minor matters had to wait.

"Let's go, " I said.

I crept forward and she kept pace just behind me, and I had to admit that she was quiet. Maybe she had grown up playing Red Indians in the woods of Oklahoma. I told my mind to stop wondering and pay attention to the job in hand.

The undergrowth was like a strangled green maze that nature in a joking mood had tied into ravelled knots. I eased my way through and the leaves caressed or scratched at my bare shoulders. My heart began to thump again because I was sure that I must be almost on top of that guard at the entrance to the bunker below, and I forgot all about Evelyn Ryan. I had to concentrate on silencing that little man with AK–47 before he became aware of my presence.

I moved more branches aside with careful fingers and threaded my body through the gap. I listened, heard nothing close, and gingerly inched my way forward again. I was crouching, with my buttocks touching my heels, and my fingertips balanced against the damp earth. Then I heard a distinct sound that was practically under my nose.

I lowered my weight on to the palms of my hands and slowly shifted my balance forward. My head emerged from a clump of long grass and immediately ahead was the open clearing, and beyond the network of footpaths that led back to the cove. I looked downwards and my face was less than twelve inches from the top of a wide cone of plaited straw; a coolie hat, and underneath it the Viet Cong guard.

I was so close that he had to sense my presence. I spared only a fleeting glance to ensure that none of his comrades were in sight, and then I reached down and grabbed him with both hands, one hand hooked under his chin and the other gripping the back of his neck. I hoisted him up bodily with barely a squawk and dragged him back on to the grass beside me. He dropped his rifle into the tunnel mouth below and his legs flailed wildly in the air. I kept my left hand clamped tight under his chin to keep his mouth shut, and with my right I swept his coolie hat away. His bulging eyes were terrified but this was no time for mercy. I smashed my clenched fist down like a club squarely between them, and they glazed over and the light of fear went out.

I dropped him back into the narrow trench and jumped down after him. With one hand I scooped up his fallen rifle but my haste was unnecessary. For the moment there were no more Viet Cong in sight.

Evelyn Ryan slithered down into the trench beside me without waiting for any help, bringing with her a rain of dirt and clumps of grass. She gave me a conspirator's grin.

"Well done, Mister Steele."

"John," I said. "If our Vietnamese Mata Hari can call me Johnny then so can you!"

I was already towing our unconscious friend deeper into the tunnel with my left hand knotted around the shoulder material of his black cotton shirt. I had to duck my head and bend almost double as I moved backwards, and Evelyn stooped to pick up the guard's trailing legs and give me a hand. We dumped him just a few yards inside where he would be out of sight, and then I had the difficult task of turning my body round to face the way I wanted to go. The Viet Cong didn't even dig their bunkers so that they could stand up straight.

I was practically on my knees as I moved deeper into the earth, and Evelyn crouched close behind me. The AK-47 was ready in my hands. We were blotting out the daylight and had to grope our way blindly. The tunnel burrowed downwards and then turned a corner.

Ten yards ahead was a faint glimmer of light, the only sign that the tunnel continued in that direction. I moved towards it, and even with my knees and back bent I bumped my head on the low roof. My shoulders wedged for a moment between the narrowing earth walls and suddenly I knew what claustrophobia meant. My sweat ran cold but I kept going, and I sensed that there were more openings on either side that we could not see. I could only hope that there was nobody inside those invisible chambers to hear us pass. I could feel

Evelyn touching my back, and then she found my belt and held on.

The light came from two paraffin lamps in the large square chamber at the end of the tunnel. One lamp was suspended from the centre of a bamboo beam stretched across the low ceiling, while the other was standing on a small wooden table that also supported a map case, some half open maps and a neat pile of clean rice bowls. The walls of the chamber were shored up with bamboo, and there was no doubt in my mind that we had found the Viet Cong underground HQ. We had also found what we had come to seek, for on the far side of the chamber was a second table, on which stood a large radio transmitter.

There was only one man in the bunker, the radio operator who sat with his back to us before his seat. I was half-way across the room before he jumped up and turned and I jabbed him smartly in the belly with the combat rifle.

"Hold still," I snapped, and motioned him to stand aside.

His face was startled but he was an intelligent coward. He scuttled sideways and put his hands up over his head.

"Cover him," I said, and gave the rifle to Evelyn Ryan.

I sat down quickly before the radio and pulled on the headphones. Then I stared at the incomprehensible Chinese characters that marked the dials and wavebands. The set was obviously a gift from Red China, and all that I could do was to twiddle the knobs and hope. I flicked a switch that was situated roughly where the transmit switch ought to be, turned the wavelength dial half an inch and began to pray for luck and speak rapidly all at the same time.

"Mayday . . . Mayday . . . Mayday . . ." I started off with the international distress call. "This is the MV *Shantung* calling. We have been hijacked by Viet Cong. The ship is now anchored off Hon Lai Island. Latitude—"

101

Faintly we heard the sound of shouting voices some-where outside.

"Hurry, John," Evelyn urged. "There are three exits to this room. We haven't a hope of holding them off!"

She was right. They could come at us three ways at once and it sounded as though the uproar had already started. If the call was picked up then the location Hon Lai Island would have to be enough. I skipped the lati-tude and longitude and I didn't waste time listening for any acknowledgement. I just turned the wavelength dial.

"Mayday . . . Mayday . . . Mayday . . . This is the MV *Shantung* calling. We have been hijacked by Viet Cong. The ship is now anchored off Hon Lai Island."

Another twist of the dial and now the uproar was ominously close. I could visualize men racing up fast from the beach.

"Mayday . . . Mayday . . . Mayday . . ."

I got it off twice more before Evelyn shouted a warn-ing and opened fire down one of the tunnels. The AK–47 sounded like a machine gun in the confined space, but to cover one tunnel she had to turn her back on two others and the radio operator. He wasn't such a complete coward after all because the moment the rifle was no longer pointing to his middle he jumped her.

I sprang up and plucked him off her back, and as I swung him round he got out a fast, screeching jabber in Vietnamese before I knocked him cold. I should have done that in the first place and now it was too late. His comrades were already rushing us from three sides and that one shout was enough to bring the whole horde down upon our necks. Evelyn lost the rifle and the des-perate fight that I tried to put up from a half kneeling position was a doomed effort. I lasted only a minute but I heard her retreat behind me and make a last desperate appeal into the radio.

"Mayday . . . Mayday . . . Mayday . . ."

Her voice was still echoing in my brain as the rifle butts started to strike home and I was beaten uncon-scious by a dozen irate little men. They were a sea of cursing yellow faces and slitted eyes, and I tried to give Evelyn another few seconds before they got past me.

The darkness was a sweet, drowning relief from pain.

I came back to the world of pain with sunlight streaming into my eyes, but now it was a dull pain, the aftermath of pain and not the execution of the pain itself. I was lying on my back, and when I tried to open my eyes the hot sun blinded me. I felt as though my whole body was one big, wincing bruise.

I was hauled into a sitting position where I had to blink a few times, and then I saw the yellow robe—the symbol of peace and humility that I had come to hate as the newly perverted symbol of arrogance. Thang was standing over me, and although his eyes were radiating fury he managed to combine a grate of malicious pleasure into his voice.

"You failed," he said. "Do you understand that, Chief Officer—you failed! The radio set was switched to receive, not to transmit. You should learn to read Chinese!"

I said nothing. There was no point in getting bitter over what at best had only been a fifty-fifty gamble. I looked for Evelyn Ryan and found her standing upright among the ring of armed guerillas who surrounded me. Two of the black-garbed little men were holding fast to her arms, and she looked white-faced and shaken. She had taken a beating too, for I could count the fresh bruises.

"Did they hurt you too much?" I asked.

"Not as much as they hurt you." She tried to keep her voice steady, but then it began to break. "John, it was my cabin that they found empty. Thang raised the alarm to search for me, they didn't even know that you were ashore. John, I'm sorry. I've made a mess of it again."

She was hurt and near to tears, so this time I had to be generous.

"Perhaps it will be third time lucky," I said. "Don't give up." I managed to struggle to my feet and my arms were seized from behind as I glowered at Thang. "And maybe this little rat is lying to us anyway. If we were transmitting he wouldn't let us have the satisfaction of knowing that we just might have got a message out."

"Enough!"

Thang closed the conversation without argument, which meant that he had no worries on that score. He hadn't been lying. He lifted the combat rifle in his hand and pointed through the trees towards the masked *Shantung*.

"We will return to the ship. Our work is finished and tonight the ship will sail again. You will plot a new course for another island—the island of Hon San."

Hon San meant no more to me than Hon Lai had done when I first heard it, but it meant something to Evelyn Ryan. I saw the flash of recognition that registered briefly in her eyes.

CHAPTER ELEVEN

FOR the rest of that day the *Shantung* lay in peace and
the island itself might have been no more than an un-
spoiled bird sanctuary. I was taken back to my cabin
and confined there in isolation under extra guards.
Hong was still pretending to be asleep in my bunk when
we returned and Thang's men hustled him out. They
returned my shirt and cap with a few additional bloodstains, and much later when the unfortunate steward
served my next meal I saw that he too bore the marks
of a beating. I could only apologize but he bore no
grudge. He seemed relieved that at least they hadn't
killed him.

The long afternoon passed slowly, the heat was sti-
fling and all that I could do was to brood.

I must have slept briefly for I opened my eyes to find
that the cabin was filled with dusk shadows. The heat
was still sultry and I got up to take a shower. When I
lay back on my bunk the darkness was thickening, and I
heard the splash of steering oars in the cove and the
sounds of movement and voices. Night had fallen, and
the Viet Cong had emerged from their holes and were
returning to strip off the camouflage and prepare the
Shantung for the open sea.

Thang came for me after another hour of busy activity
on the decks, and I was marched out with three rifles at
my back and returned to the bridge. All the draped netting had been removed and ferried back to the shore
and the *Shantung* could breathe again. But she was not
the same ship, now our rusty old freighter had fighting
teeth, two heavy field pieces in the bows remained, and

the heavy Chinese machine guns were balanced upon swivel tripods on each wing of the bridge.

Ching was already there, with a quartermaster by the wheel and a seaman to operate the telegraph. He stepped forward and raised his hand in a polite salute, his usual greeting, but his face was blank beneath the peak of his cap and lacked its usual smile. He kept his feelings hidden, but I felt certain that his lips had not relaxed since David Kee had died.

"The engine room is standing by," he reported. "The Bo'sun and his men are on deck. We are ready to sail."

"Thank you, Mister Ching."

I returned his salute because it was routine respect, and because it ignored and offended Thang. I walked to the front of the bridge and looked down into the bows.

Ho Wan was at his post, arms folded and stolidly waiting, but Thang was taking no chances in allowing me to have both my key officers on deck at the same time. I calculated that he had been reinforced by at least a platoon of fresh Viet Cong guerillas who lounged around the rails and were obviously sailing with us, plus the artillery units and the two-man teams who stood by the machine guns. The men that I had on deck were out-numbered by ten to one, and any hope of resistance was now further away than ever.

"The ship will sail!" Thang commanded.

I made him wait for another thirty seconds just to maintain a minimum of face, and then gave the necessary orders.

The engines started to turn and build up their buried power, the anchor rattled aboard, and then the propeller began to bite in reverse. Like some creaking, steel-plated slug the *Shantung* began to move backwards, and in very slow motion I nursed her stern first out of the cove. The walls of jungle now looked solid and black and more menacing, but we withdrew safely, and just a few of the sampans came out to wave us goodbye.

As we cleared the cove Lin Chi came up on to the bridge again. She wore her white silk trousers and a powder blue tunic, and her black hair was re-tied into a neat pony tail. She refrained from looking at my battered face and stood back out of the way while I completed the task of maneuvring the *Shantung* out into safe water, then she turned and went into the chart room and switched on the light. Thang motioned me to follow her.

I handed the bridge over to Ching and told him to hold the ship steady on stop engines. There was no current and no wind.

In the chart room Lin Chi pointed out our next port of call. It was another island, about three times the size of Hon Lai and some fifty miles further out to sea and to the north.

"This is Hon San," she said. "You will take the ship there."

"And what happens when we get there?"

"No questions," Thang said. He was behind me again. "You will find out when we arrive."

I couldn't argue. I computed the course and then returned to the bridge.

"Slow ahead engines," I ordered. "Mister Ching, hard to starboard and then bring the ship round to eighty degrees east by south. That's your new course."

"And you will maintain full speed," Thang said. "How long before we reach Hon San."

I shrugged. "At twelve knots about four hours. The *Shantung* isn't a speedboat."

Thang smiled. "Plenty of time before dawn. It will do."

I watched the ship change course under Ching's direction, the bows swinging almost full circle under a night sky that was once more scattered with the galaxies and constellations I knew so well. Soon the dark bulk of Hon Lai was directly behind us and Ching ordered full ahead on the new course. I tasted the breeze and was disappointed. It was a calm night with no hope of a storm.

Typhoons were like policemen, there was never one around when you really needed them

Lin Chi moved past me and went out on to the port

wing of the bridge. There she leaned against the rail, a silent and troubled young woman. I waited half an hour while the ship ploughed ahead at her steady rate of twelve knots, and then Thang decided that all was sufficiently under control for him to attend to other matters. Perhaps he had a briefing or a pep talk to give, for he called Dinh up on to the bridge to take his place and then went below.

I made no move for another five minutes, and then I strolled idly out on to the wing. Dinh watched me go but made no protest and none of the other guards seemed disturbed. I leaned against the rail beside Lin Chi. We gazed together at the stars.

"Half of them are still yours," I said at last.

She looked at me then, and her black eyes were glistening. I wondered if crocodile tears could possibly last that long.

"They brought Evelyn Ryan back to the saloon," she said. "She told me what happened. Johnny, you should not have gone ashore. Why must you try to fight us?"

"You've played pirates with my ship," I reminded her. "What else can I do?"

She didn't answer and I looked out over the darkened sea and allowed another minute to go by.

"What will we find at Hon San?" I asked.

She hesitated and I turned my head back to meet her eyes.

"We'll be there in a little over three hours, and then I shall probably find out anyway. Thang just enjoys denying me any answers. You can tell me now." I smiled wryly and finished: "It's a small return for half the stars in the sky."

"Johnny!" She touched my arm as though I had hurt her, and then she slowly nodded her head.

"All right, I will tell you. Hon San is a prison island. You have perhaps heard of Devil's Island, where France once marooned all of her dangerous convicts. Well, Hon San is a very similar sort of place. It was turned into a prison island by the French in the colonial days, and it was there that they sent all the Vietnamese who tried to oppose their rule. You must know that there were many rebellions by the Vietnamese people. The French were cruel masters, much worse than your own English colonialists, and they ran Indo-China for profit only and cared nothing for the natives. Now they have bequeathed Hon San to the present rulers of South Vietnam, and they use it in turn to hold the people whom they class as political prisoners."

I looked around at all our new armaments, and at the waiting men with their combat rifles and sub-machine guns who sat around the hatches on the well deck, and now it was all clear.

"So you've got yourself a five-minute navy," I said. "And now you're going to make a surprise commando raid on that island and release all the prisoners. Is that it?"

She nodded. "Yes, Johnny, that is it."

There was still a missing piece to the jigsaw and I pressed her further.

"Why are you here? You don't fit into all this—so why are you part of it?"

She hesitated, and her knuckles grew white where she gripped the rail.

"I told you once about my father," she said slowly. "Do you remember? He is a professor of languages, a mandarin scholar. He is a very wise and kind old man. He is a prisoner on Hon San island. He has been there for three years and I know his health is broken. They intend him to rot, and I must help him before he dies."

Now I was really beginning to understand, and I knew at last that the small tear that found its way down her cheek was genuine. I moved my hand and covered hers on the rail.

"I'm sorry," I said. "Is your father a Communist?"

"No!" She was suddenly angry at the suggestion and withdrew her hand from mine. "My father is a man of peace and he tried to stay neutral between the two sides. He tried to suggest to the rulers of South Vietnam that they should compromise with the Communist Vietnamese—who are our people also—and to make peace instead of war. They said that his politics were foolish and dangerous and for that they threw him into Hon

109

San. In Vietnam all men of peace who try to view the problem without favor to either side are automatically classed with the Communists."

"It's a rough world," I said, because it was true.

She nodded and quietened a little.

"There are I think three hundred prisoners in the camp on Hon San. Perhaps two hundred and fifty are dedicated Communists. The others are intellectuals, men who have tried to stay neutral and seek peace like my father, and of course many of them are Buddhists. Some of them are priests."

"I thought the Buddhist philosophy was non-involvement?"

"It is—but in Vietnam all of our political leaders who would normally be in opposition to the Government have been eliminated. Many people only have faith in their religious leaders, and some of those priests have seen their religious leadership as the only alternative to the two present choices that face Vietnam—the choice of Communism or an eternal civil war under the patronage of the United States. Some of the priests have long been seeking for peace outside the pagodas."

"That explains the old monk."

"You mean Huynh Quoc?" She nodded. "He is a friend of my father, as I have told you. He has always been our family priest when we visited the pagoda in Hue. And some of the priests who are held on Hon San with my father are also his friends." She paused and told me what I had already known. "Huynh Quoc is a very disturbed man. He is a good man and his spirit is torn with agony. He has strayed further from the Path than he ever intended."

I said softly: "And you are a very disturbed woman. You should never have come this far either."

"I had to come," she answered, "for my father."

We were silent for a moment, watching the stars, and when I replaced my hand over her own she didn't withdraw.

"Thang and his men don't intend to release just your father and the men of peace," I said at last. "They're more interested in freeing the hardened Communists,

110

giving them new arms and letting them loose on the mainland again."

"That's why we had to come this far, Huynh Quoc and I—we have to be sure that my father and the others like him are not left behind."

I could see the pitfall into which they had been led and said quietly:

"And I suppose you had to use Section Leader Thang and his Viet Cong?"

"Yes." She looked at me helplessly. "It was our plan, mine and Huynh Quoc's, but how can a girl and one old monk capture a ship and then invade an island? We had to have help and we could only turn to the National Liberation Front. It took many weeks for Huynh Quoc to make contact with the Northern Zonal Central Committee, and they passed us on to the Central Committee for the Saigon sector. They approved our plan and gave us Thang and his unit."

"I guess they must have tried to compensate for any softness in yourself and the monk—they picked you a right bunch of thugs."

"Thang is a soldier," she said. "He likes fighting and carrying arms, and his family were all killed in one of those accidents that happen when the American planes bomb a friendly village. That makes him bitter. He has been a Section Leader for five years, and Dinh has been his assistant for three years. Dinh is not so cold inside, but he is a natural soldier too."

She did not want to defend them any further and became silent, and I knew that she was unhappy that the real power of command had been taken over by Thang. She should have known better than to expect otherwise, but I suspected that like the old monk she had been naïve at the outset. I voiced what was in my mind.

"I'm surprised that Thang allowed you and Huynh Quoc to come along at all. I'm sure he would have preferred to do without both of you."

"He could not have his own way," Lin Chi said. "Huynh Quoc had to bring the monk guerillas aboard. And—and I too insisted that I could be useful."

"By seducing me at the right moment!"

111

My rancour smarted again, and she turned to me with a new surge of emotion.

"Johnny, I'm sorry. I had to do that. I had to agree to it or there was no reason for me to come on this trip—and for my father's sake I have to be on board."

She gripped my arm and she was near to tears again.

"Johnny, it wasn't easy for me. It was the first time I have been with a man. And then you made it easy because you were gentle, and then it was all wrong because I was cheating you. I wanted you to be an animal, Johnny. I wanted you to hurt me because then I could hate you and it wouldn't matter. But I was afraid. And you knew it and you loved me so tenderly. And then I couldn't hate you, Johnny. And afterwards you hated me!"

The tears were coming fast now, as though they had been pent up for too long. I turned her to face me and just then I didn't care a damn for the watching machine gunners, or Dinh and his guards.

"Please don't hate me, Johnny," she begged, and her sad face glistened in the starlight.

I kissed her lips, as gently as before.

"I understand," I said. "And that's how much I hate you."

After she had run below I stayed at the rail, letting my thoughts race and swirl where they pleased. I couldn't even begin to sort them out into any coherent order. Two hours passed and I was startled out of my reverie when Ching approached.

"We're closing in on the island, Mister Steele. I think that's it on the horizon."

He offered me a pair of night glasses and I sighted them for a moment into the darkness beyond the bows. I could just detect the low smudge of deeper blackness that had to be Hon San, and I nodded in agreement. I hadn't noticed Thang return to the bridge, but he too emerged from the wheelhouse and used a pair of glasses. Then he swung round on me.

"Stop the ship, and put out all lights."

I nodded to Ching and he walked back into the wheelhouse.

"Stop engines," he commanded. "And then switch off the lights."

The telegraph jangled, and slowly the *Shantung* lost way and began to roll slightly in the long swell. The navigation lights went out, and then the lights in the wheelhouse as the duty seamen moved around flicking switches. Ching came out to rejoin me and we stood in darkness.

Thang was searching the sea on our port bow and so I raised my glasses again and followed his example. On the second sweep I saw the glimmer of a signal light far out on the ocean.

Thang snapped an order and Dinh moved forward with a large torch. He flashed the beam quickly three times and then waited. After a minute two answering flashes came back. Dinh smiled in the gloom and Thang relaxed.

"What does it all mean?" I asked.

Thang turned slowly and I thought that he was going to utter his routine, *no questions,* but we were too close to our target and he decided that it was time for at least one explanation.

"It means that all is well, Chief Officer, and that for a short time we must be patient and wait. Out there on the ocean there are six large sea-going junks, all carrying extra commando units of our comrades. One junk is now moving inshore to land the first unit in the swamps to the north of Hon San island. The task of that unit will be to make their way through the swamps and attack from behind to destroy the radio link that the island has with the mainland. That will also be the signal for the remaining junks and for this ship to launch our main attack."

He smiled briefly. "The small harbour on this island is defended by three 155 millimetre artillery pieces, but you will sail into the teeth of those guns so that the gun teams we have installed in the bows of this ship can knock them out. We shall have surprise on our side, for they have never really expected that this island could be attacked. And when the time comes, Chief Officer, you and your ship have the honour of leading our assault force."

CHAPTER TWELVE

THERE was nothing to do but wait, and the *Shantung* and all on board seemed to lie in a sea-bound vacuum of suspense and anticipation, like a ghost ship with a phantom crew. The engines still throbbed gently, muffled below decks while the ship lay idle, and the rolling motion grew more positive as the long swell heaved in from the north east. The starlight was sufficient to reveal the silhouettes of the bridge structure and the silent, armed men, and beyond the bows it gave a faint phosphorescence to the salt lacework that crested the waves.

The flotilla of junks that we knew were present were invisible in the night, and the dark sea gave the impression of emptiness on our port bow. Directly ahead was the smudged distortion of the horizon that I might possibly have mistaken for a bank of low cloud if I had not known that it was the island of Hon San, and I tried to visualize that lone junk landing the initial party of saboteurs in the swamps. They would have to be a suicide party of volunteer fanatics, for even if they succeeded in their objective they would then have raised the alarm and be at the mercy of the island's defenders for too long before the main assault force could come to their aid.

If they failed to silence the island's radio station then we could all expect a flight of angry US Skyhawks from the nearest aircraft carrier howling around our ears. One yelp of what was happening would have the planes overhead in minutes, and then the Viet Cong's brand new five-minute navy would be lucky to survive for fifty seconds. At every stage in this operation the key factor was the radio.

I had remained standing on the wing of the bridge and Ching stayed at my side. Thang and Dinh had moved away into the wheelhouse to converse in low tones, and no one seemed to be unduly worried over what I might have to say to my Third Officer. They were too confident that there was nothing we could do.

After a few moments Ching asked quietly:

"Can they succeed?"

"If the man in charge of that landing party is as ruthless as Thang the answer is probably yes."

"And we have to help them?"

Now that we were shrouded in darkness some of his carefully concealed bitterness was coming to the surface in his voice.

I said softly: "We have to remember Captain Butcher's advice."

"What was that?"

"A couple of chess rules he gave me. The game isn't over until it's won, so even though you're losing you keep playing. We have to be ready to take advantage of any opportunity, or any mistake that Thang makes."

Ching complimented our enemy reluctantly.

"I do not think that Section Leader Thang will make any mistakes."

"Neither do I, but there may still be opportunities. If we could take over these machine guns we could dominate the bridge and as we sail into Hon San under fire we may get the chance. If it happens I intend to be in a position to rush the port wing. If you can take the starboard—"

I didn't finish because there was a sudden shout, a scuffle and a sharp cry of pain from the starboard side of the darkened boatdeck behind us. We both turned sharply and I saw Thang run out of the far side of the wheelhouse and clatter quickly down the companionway with Dinh behind him.

"Stay here," I told Ching, and then I hurried after them.

One of the remaining guards tried to stop me, but

116

there had been a shrill, feminine note to that cry of pain and I swept him aside. He could have shot me dead but he knew that my life at the moment was worth more than his own, and he could only swallow his frustration and hurry behind me.

I went down the companionway in one rapid slide with both hands braced on the rails, and my feet hit the boatdeck only a few yards behind the two guerilla leaders. The creator of the disturbance and the cause of their anger was struggling between two more of the monk guerillas, and I recognized the familiar freckles and the chestnut brown hair.

They were fighting under the first of the two starboard lifeboats, but Evelyn became still as Thang and Dinh arrived. Thang was snarling in Vietnamese, and one of the two men who had apprehended the girl showed him the fat-barrelled flare pistol he had taken from her hand. I recognized it as part of the lifeboats's standard equipment, it was used to fire brilliant red or green distress signals into the sky.

Thang was livid with rage.

"So you would have warned our enemies on Hon San!"

He screamed at her. "You would have betrayed us! This is the third time you have tried to stop our mission and I will tolerate no more. You will die!"

He raised his combat rifle and would have pulled the trigger but I thrust myself between them.

"That's enough!" I threw his own favourite phrase into his teeth. "If she dies then I refuse to sail this ship another inch."

There was blind fury in his slitted eyes and he tried to ram the barrel of his rifle hard into my middle. I clamped both hands on the cold steel, checking the blow and then holding fast. Dinh cocked his own rifle automatically at my chest.

"Stand aside," Thang said. "Stand aside, Chief Officer, or I will kill you too."

"And then who do you get to sail the ship?"

Thang was trembling, too infuriated to speak, and it

117

was Dinh who answered. The little man was very steady and careful now.

"The Third Officer will sail the ship."

I nodded. "Sure my Third Officer can sail the ship— on the open sea!" I ignored Dinh and met Thang's blazing eyes again. "James Ching is a damned good junior officer. In twenty years time he'll be a Chief Officer, and in thirty years time he will very likely be Captain of his own ship. But not tonight! Tonight he's just a young man with very limited experience. There's only one man aboard who can take the *Shantung* into an unknown harbor straight down the throat of those three guns you mentioned—and that man is me!"

There was an icy silence. Thang had two choices, to kill me or to back down. He was a fanatic, but I believed that the success of his mission meant more to him than saving his own face, and without me he couldn't take the *Shantung* into Hon San. For thirty seconds we faced each other over the combat rifle, and I thought that I had misjudged him and that I was going to die. My brain was cold, and either way it didn't matter because for me there had only been the one choice. I couldn't have stood aside to watch while a brave girl was murdered before my eyes.

Then, very slowly, Thang drew back. I released my grip on the barrel of his rifle and the chilled steel slid through my fingers. The muzzle steadied again still only twelve inches from my navel, but I forced myself to relax.

"Very well," Thang said. "In return for your cooperation the girl will be allowed to live. But I will tolerate no more! She will be taken below, and my men will have orders to shoot her dead if they believe that she is even thinking of some new trick."

I nodded, and then turned to look at Evelyn Ryan. Her face was paler than death and I guessed that her stomach must feel equally as ill as mine. She had to swallow hard before she could speak.

"I'm sorry again, John. You said don't give up, and third time lucky, but I guess it wasn't."

"At least you had an idea that I hadn't already covered," I said. "I'd forgotten all about the flare pistols."

She said nothing and she couldn't smile, but her eyes conveyed that she was grateful for that small consolation. At least I wasn't bawling her out for getting in my way. At the same time I had to introduce a note of severity into my voice.

"But now you do have to give up. Thang means what he says—and so do I! *No more tricks*. You must stay alive, and that's an order."

"Yes, John."

She kept her eyes downcast and sounded unexpectedly obedient, and I didn't know whether I should believe her or not. After three good tries she should have had her courage dampened or knocked out of her, but with this girl I had the feeling that the spark would never be fully extinguished.

"Take her below," Thang said harshly.

The two men who were holding her obeyed and she was led away, meekly enough, and I had to return to the bridge with my doubts.

There was no opportunity to continue my conversation with Ching, for now Thang stayed very close to my back. We waited for another half hour in the hushed and pregnant darkness, and then a violent explosion on Hon San marked the distant horizon with a flash of fiery light. It faded slowly into a flushed glow of burning and the sound of automatic gunfire echoed faintly across the black surface of the sea.

"The signal!" Thang snapped. "Take the ship in, Chief Officer."

His rifle jabbed me under the ribs, warning me that I could not hope to win another argument.

"Full ahead engines," I said calmly.

The telegraph rang down the signal and the *Shantung* shuddered like some rusty old mongrel on a leash. Jean Pierre was in command of the engine room and was immediately responsive to every clang of the bell. The ship began to push forward, butting her nose into the long seas, but now the swell had turned our bows southward as we had lain idle and we were no longer on course.

"Hard to port!"

I moved to stand at the helmsman's shoulder as he spun the wheel and watched the bows and the compass.

"Steady on seventy-five degrees."

The helmsman stopped the wheel, and our bows were aimed at the dying glow that was all that was visible of the island. The ship was thrusting hard ahead and the men on the foredeck were running to their places. The gun crews were already in position.

"I have studied maps of the island," Thang said beside me. "The radio station was at the inner end of the harbour. Keep to the course you are on now and that fire will act as a beacon to lead you into the harbour itself."

"Thank you," I said sourly. "I was beginning to wonder when you were going to give me enough information to navigate the ship. Helmsman, steady on your course!"

I looked to the night sky, where the stars were now partly obscured by high cloud. If that radio station had succeeded in getting out an S.O.S. before it had been blown up then we could soon expect company, but I couldn't count on it. I picked up the voice pipe and called Jean Pierre.

"They're using the *Shantung* to make a commando raid," I told him briefly, "so for the next hour we all either sink or swim together. I don't particularly want the *Shantung* sunk so give me everything you've got. I want this cranky old tub moving fast enough to dodge shells and aeroplanes."

"*Monsieur Steele,* you demand miracles!" His voice sounded horrified and I could picture the aghast expression on his face. "I can give you one more knot at the most."

"*Monsieur Lasalle,*" I said formally. "You will give me two if you have to blow her guts out."

"*Allez-vous-en!* I will give you one and a half and a prayer!" He paused and then: "We will do our best, Johnny."

"Thank you, Jean Pierre."

I replaced the voice pipe and waited. Half a minute

passed and then I could feel the *Shantung* strain. Her ancient steel heart was beating faster and gradually our speed increased to fourteen knots. By most standards it was in a crawl, but for the *Shantung* this was her first gallop in twenty years.

Thang was smiling beside me.

"Very good, Chief Officer, you are growing wise."

" I don't intend to let you sink my ship," I told him curtly.

I walked out on to the port wing and raised my glasses to my eyes. Thang kept pace with me, but without looking back I was aware that Ching had moved unobtrusively towards the starboard side. He stood in the opposite doorway with his hands clasped behind his back and stared grimly forward, and I wished that I had Ho Wan on deck to back him up.

From the island the exchange of gunfire rattled hot and clear, and it sounded as though the initial landing party were pinned down and hard pressed to hold their own. I stared through the glasses but I could only distinguish the red flashes of the sub-machines guns. I swept the glasses back carefully towards the sea and vaguely I could define movement. I held steady as the ship closed in and slowly the harbour wall took shape with men running desperately to and fro. I followed one group and saw them reach the first of the big guns and swing the giant barrel round to face us. Magnified through the sensitive lenses of my binoculars the muzzle looked as vast and deep as one of hell's bottomless pits.

"What's the range of those guns?"

"Twenty-five-thousand-four-hundred yards maximum," Thang replied precisely.

We were already within a mile of the shore and closing fast, and at our present speed I calculated we would ram the harbour wall in under five minutes.

"I hope they're lousy gunners," I said bleakly. "What's the range of our own hardware?"

"Twelve hundred yards." Thang remained calm.

I moved the glasses and found the two remaining long-snouted monsters defending the opposite side of the harbour. More men were milling around them and they

121

had already marked our blacked-out and headlong approach as hostile. While I watched the nearest gun opened fire, flexing its steel muscles with a mighty shudder and recoil. I lowered my glasses and listened to the bang of the explosion, and then there came the high-pitched scream of a shell and the sea burst up into a fountain of spray two hundred yards away from our port beam.

"You see, they are lousy gunners," Thang said contemptuously.

The single gun on the north side of the harbour roared as he spoke and pitched another shell over our heads to explode in our wake. The guerillas on our decks threw themselves flat or crouched in the scuppers, while the machine gunners on the bridge ducked low. Only the two gun teams in our bows remained standing. The third of the big shore guns dropped a shell short on our starboard bow, and still the men by the twenty-five pounders did not flinch.

"Helmsman, hold your course," I shouted into the wheelhouse. And then to Thang: "What's the rate of fire on those guns?"

"Two rounds per minute," he answered. "From three guns six rounds per minute. Our rate of fire is three rounds per minute. From two guns six rounds per minute. That gives us equal firing power, Chief Officer."

"But they are firing bigger shells."

"We have better gunners—and fixed targets."

Another salvo of shells cut short our argument, one behind, one way out off the starboard bow, and the third close enough to rock the ship and drench the bows with spray. Thang looked shaken and I said savagely:

"They've got at least one good gun crew."

I raised my glasses again and swept the harbor. Men were still running there as though in panic and flames still showed where the radio station burned. The gun teams were like frantic ants as they slammed fresh rounds into the breeches. I turned briefly to the sea and after a fast sweep found two of the junk flotilla racing in ahead of us on auxiliary engines. The dim creaming of their wake gave them away. I had to strain my eyes to detect the three remaining craft, but they were all there ahead of us and moving in at full speed. They had slipped closer inshore while awaiting the attack signal, but now we were overhauling them fast. The *Shantung* would hit the harbor first and we were the prime target for the guns.

The long muzzles flashed and roared again, and again the seas erupted all around us as the screaming shells crashed down. The ship pitched sideways as though tossed by a tidal wave, and then the two gun teams in our bows began to answer fire. We were well within twelve hundred yards and it was time to join battle. The two twenty-five pounders exploded with a double bang and hurled their own shells back to the shore. The ropes that held the guns secure flexed visibly with the recoil but did not break.

Three more shells from the shore guns, two wide and one dangerous near miss. The *Shantung* heaved again and shuddered under a torrential rain of spray. That was too close and I moved back to the wheelhouse door.

"Helmsman, hard to starboard."

"No! Stay on course!"

Thang countermanded my order above the noise of the second salvo from the bows, and the helmsman froze helplessly. I ran towards him and spun the wheel. The ship started to answer and then Thang was ramming the barrel of his combat rifle against the side of my throat.

"We zig-zag," I told him angrily. "You want to get there in one piece don't you?"

He hesitated. Our bows were veering away and then the next salvo of enemy shells were screaming towards us. One whine was hideously close and completed its journey with an almighty explosion at waterline on the port bow. The ship reared up under the impact and the men of both our gun teams were thrown reeling across the deck. The sea cascaded down and out through the scuppers, as the *Shantung* continued to lurch to starboard.

Thang withdrew his rifle and held back.

I feared that we had been holed but the ship surged onward without slackening speed, and I held her for thirty seconds before spinning the wheel to bring her back on seventy-five degrees. The gunners in our bows had picked themselves up and were ramming home a new round of shells as I handed the wheel back to the helmsman.

"Steady on course," I said harshly. "And you listen only for my orders!

"Aye, aye, sir!"

He had the courage to answer and I left him and hurried back to the wing. I sighted my glasses on the shore again as more shells were exchanged, and I saw that now some of the wooden harbor buildings behind the two long guns on the southside were ablaze. Our gunners were getting their range too. One of the big guns suddenly buckled sideways in an obliterating flash of flame.

Thang gave a shout of triumph from inside the wheelhouse, and the gun teams in the bows gave a ragged cheer. Then two more deafening explosions drowned them out as the remaining guns answered back. Another shell drenched the front of the ship, and I knew that one of those guns was accurately lowering elevation to keep pace with us. A fractional traverse and he would have us with a direct hit.

"Hard to port," I shouted.

The helmsman obeyed and Thang did not interfere. The ship swung round and the next near miss was on our starboard flank.

"Hard to starboard!"

I wondered how many times I could outwit that gun team and now the sweat was sticky along my spine. I sighted with the glasses again and saw the shore gun on the north side recoil. Our gunners were still concentrating on the remaining gun on the south side as the shell whistled towards us. It exploded on the port bow close enough to throw them sprawling again.

"Helmsman, steady as you are! Hold that course!"

It was time to break the zig-zag pattern before that shore crew got wise and dropped one hundred pounds of high explosive into our laps, and I prayed that it was the right order.

Ten seconds passed. The south gun boomed and flashed with a wide miss behind us. Another twenty seconds and the north gun belched again. I gritted my teeth as the shell scream sounded and then it blew up a mighty jet of water forty yards from our port bow. If my last order had been hard to port he would have scored a direct hit, and now I had to out-guess him again.

"Hard to port!"

The helmsman hesitated and I shouted again savagely:

"Damn you, *Hard to port!*"

He spun the wheel and I ran forward to the rail. Our guns recoiled with a reverberating double bang and I cupped my hands to my mouth and roared:

"You're aiming for the wrong bloody gun! It's the north gun that's getting close!".

If they heard they didn't understand, but Dinh was standing alert on the wing of the bridge and he pressed instantly to my side. He shouted out in Vietnamese and one of the gunners turned. Dinh leaned forward and shouted again at the top of his voice and received a hand gesture of acknowledgement. Orders were shouted in the bows and the muzzles of both field pieces began to traverse rapidly to port. Dinh drew back from the rail and grinned at me faintly.

"The north gun, Chief Officer, okay?"

"Okay," I said.

The shore guns flashed and hurled two more shells. We were within half a mile and the south gun still hadn't found the right elevation, but the north gun again blew a hole in the sea on our starboard bow. The helmsman gave me a desperate look and now I had to gamble blind.

"Steady as you are. Hold your course."

Our luck ran out. It was only a matter of time and I knew that I was wrong as soon as I heard the next shell shrieking towards us. The pitch was higher and instinctively I turned away and threw myself flat. The shell

125

struck the foredeck at the base of the bridge and exploded with a fearsome sheet of flame. The sound was a violent agony in my eardrums and the *Shantung* was hurled to starboard like some gallant old lady taking a killer punch from the heavy-weight champion of the world.

It was what I had feared and what I had waited for. There was not a man left standing on the bridge and I was the first to scramble to my knees and pick myself up. There was screaming from the dying men on the foredeck and a frenzy of voices, and above it the crackle of fire and burning. The glass had shattered in all the wheelhouse windows but I did not stop to glance into the wheelhouse itself. The *Shantung* was turning helplessly out of control but for the moment I abandoned the ship.

I made a run for the machine gun balanced on the wing of the bridge.

Dinh was regaining his feet and groping for his combat rifle, and then he sensed what was happening and tried to get in my way. I hooked him under the jaw with a vicious right cross and sent him spinning again and continued my race along the bridge. The two machine gunners were stunned and one of them crouched on his knees. The second man tried to haul himself up behind the tripod of the gun and swung the barrel round to meet me. I knocked it back with a frantic sweep of my arm and then I grabbed him and flung him bodily out of the way. The guerilla on his knees pushed himself up in a weak spring but I drove my right fist hard into his skinny belly. He crashed back and I was behind the gun. I swung it triumphantly to cover the bridge and then I froze with my finger round the trigger.

Ching hadn't made it. He was standing dazed and helpless in the wheelhouse doorway, and his face dripped with blood where the flying glass from the broken window had cut him open above the right eye. He would have fallen except that Thang was holding him up by one shoulder, with a combat rifle acting as a second prop. Thang looked shaken but he hadn't been hurt at all.

126

"Enough, Chief Officer! Come away from that machine gun or your friend will be the first to die!"

I said slowly: "I could kill you both. At least you would die too!"

"And for what purpose? You are a fool, Chief Officer. If we fight among ourselves those shore guns will destroy us all."

He was right and I knew it. If Ching had captured the second machine gun then we would have had complete control of the bridge and perhaps a fighting chance. Now I was not a match for all the fire-power that could be brought against me, and Thang was using Ching as a human shield. I saw Dinh crawl tentatively along the deck and reach out one hand to retrieve his AK-47, but it made no difference. I couldn't open fire on my own Third Officer.

I pushed the shoulder rest of the machine gun up and let the muzzle swing down to point harmlessly at the deck, and then I stepped out from behind it and walked back to the wheelhouse. Thang allowed Ching to slump to the ground and stepped back with his rifle levelled.

The seaman who had operated the telegraph was unconscious on the deck, but the helmsman was back on his feet, supporting himself against the wheel and shaking his head.

"Hard to starboard!" I snapped.

One tack was as good as the other now but he nodded and obeyed. I moved forward as though nothing had happened, ignoring Thang, and surveyed the damage. There were half a dozen dead and wounded guerillas scattered across the foredeck immediately below, and there was a gaping hole like an open mouth of fire where the shell had landed. All of the nearer deck was a shambles although in the bows the two gun teams had rallied and were again pumping shells at the shore. The scene was a chaos of smoke and flame and noise that shattered the senses.

Another whining scream, and another shell spurting up the sea on our port bow.

"Hard to port!"

I turned to Thang and added bluntly:

127

"Get my Bo'sun on deck to handle that fire. Your men don't even know where to start."

He nodded and shouted to Dinh who hurried below. The mutiny was over and we both knew that we had to work together again.

I had lost count of the seconds between the flashes now and simply gave a jumble of orders with no pattern as the shells from the two shore guns rained all around us. The *Shantung* twisted and danced as I brought her rushing in towards the harbour mouth, and I waited tensed for another direct hit. I raised my glasses and watched the exploding flashes of our own shells falling around that northern gun, and I guessed that we were rattling their nerves. Another near miss drenched the front of the ship with spray again, and for the northern gun it was the last shot. A shell from one of our own field pieces landed smack in the middle of the shore gun team and the explosion toppled the big gun forwards.

A jubilant cry went up from our bows, and immediately the muzzles of the two field pieces turned to tackle that last remaining gun. They pounded it with six shells in a minute and when I focused my glasses on the southern side of the harbour I saw that the third gun was silent, and the only surviving gun team had fled.

"Helmsman, steady on seventy-five degrees."

I gave the order as the mouth of the harbour loomed around us and then looked briefly for Ching. He was upright again, swaying slightly and wiping the blood from his face.

"Mister Ching, stand by the telegraph."

He nodded and stumbled forward to take the place of the seaman who still lay stretched out on the deck.

The buildings along the harbour were all blazing merrily now, the flames casting a red glow over the darkened sea and giving me plenty of light to manœuvre. Our guns were the only heavy weapons now firing, systematically plastering the whole shore-line, and as we came within two hundred yards of the harbour wall the machine guns on each wing of the bridge opened fire.

"Reverse engines!"

Ching pulled the telegraph back and the bell jangled.

I felt the ship's heart stop beating momentarily as we continued to surge forward, and then the screw began to churn backwards. Slowly the *Shantung* lost momentum and was dragged to a halt.

"Hard to port."

The bows swung into the left-hand side of the harbour where a few men were still running frantically to escape the merciless fury of automatic fire that the massed guerillas were now pouring out from our decks. I waited a few seconds and strove to ignore the death and destruction on shore. I was just glad that the harbour wall was constructed from wood and not concrete.

"Hard to starboard!"

The ship swung her bows again with her port side broadside on to the harbour wall.

"Helmsman, steady as you are. Slow ahead engines."

The telegraph jangled. The ship stopped straining backwards and nudged forward.

"Reverse engines!"

The ship dragged to a stop again and it was too late to do any more.

"Stop engines!"

I waited and gripped the rail as the *Shantung* crashed violently against the harbour wall, like a full back delivering a massive shoulder charge. There was a thunderous creaking and breaking of timbers, and I gritted my teeth and winced. For a moment I was convinced that both the ship and the harbour must sink to the bottom of the small bay.

Ching was thrown off his feet again, and even Thang was pitched to his knees. On the foredeck the massed guerillas had collapsed like an army of drunks but they recovered quickly. With combat rifles and sub-machine guns blazing they jumped over the side on to the sagging harbour wall and surged forward like well-trained marines. Behind us the junks were bringing in their additional landing parties and the final storming of Hon San had begun.

We had arrived with a vengeance.

CHAPTER THIRTEEN

THE invasion and capture of Han Son was a Viet Cong affair, and I had no time to spare it any thought or concern. I had my own problem with another fire raging aboard my ship. Ching was still weak and dizzy from loss of blood and I had to order him down to the saloon where I hoped that someone would stitch up the cut above his eye; but Ho Wan was released with the Chinese crew and we battled the flames together for the next three hours. It was dawn, with bars of grey light breaking the eastern sky before we brought the blaze under control, and by then the sounds of gunfire had ceased on the island.

The Viet Cong had won their battle too, and were making prisoners of the men who had once been prison guards. The US Air Force had failed to appear, and so obviously the initial landing party who had knocked out the radio station had performed a successful job. I wondered if any of them had survived.

I stood back on the foredeck and wiped the mixture of sweat and soot from my face. I was filthy and felt as though all my muscles had been put through a mangle and crushed to pulp. The crewmen still manning the hose-pipes were also blackened and weary, but none of us looked such a mess as the ship. The superstructure of the bridge was charred and half burned away, and some of the buckled metalwork still glowed dull red. Half of the deck and the hatch cover were missing, and what remained was mostly charcoal and bloodstains.

Ho Wan was taking charge of what was left of the operation, looking like a cross between a Chinese brigand and a pig-tailed coal miner. I felt beaten but I knew that the Bo'sun still had untapped resources of strength and I could leave him to cope. The *Shantung,* for what she was worth in her present state, was saved.

I turned slowly to Thang who was standing well back by the rail behind me. Dinh was on the bridge, which was now dangerously near to collapse, and the rest of their original unit were standing guard duty. The invasion had been the business of the junk units and the one landing party we had carried.

"Let's go below," I said. "I want to see what sort of a mess I've got in the saloon."

Thang nodded without argument. His mission had been a success and there was nothing that I could do to take that away from him. Now he could afford to relax and be more pliant.

We went down to the saloon and as I feared it was a shambles. The wounded Viet Cong who had been caught in the shell blast had been carried below by the men of the two gun teams and the saloon had been transformed into a crude hospital. The Captain now shared his table with two badly mangled little yellow men, and the chairs had all been thrown out to make room for a dozen casualties stretched out on the floor. More shattered little Vietnamese sat or squatted, or merely slumped around the walls, still unbandaged and reeking of blood. I realized that they had been torn open by bullets, and that they were the unlucky ones from the landing parties.

Howard and Janet Deakin moved among them with their sleeves rolled up, working quietly and methodically. Hong had attached himself to Janet, willingly carrying bowls and fetching bandages and Evelyn Ryan was helping the missionary. They all paused and looked up wearily as Thang and I stopped in the doorway.

"The fire is out." That was all that I could tell them. I looked slowly around the mutilated bodies. "You've had a rough time."

Howard straightened up and nodded. His face was waxen under his spectacles and he looked unsteady, and yet somehow he had found strength when it was needed most. Suffering pained him more than most men, because he would never be able to turn away from it.

"We've had rough times before," he said. "It was often like this in Vietnam. You learn that there's only one thing to do, and that is that however limited you are you have to try and help them. You can't help by turning away to weep."

Janet Deakin pushed a limp strand of grey hair away from her faded eyes, and said sadly:

"They need a hospital. Half of them are going to die."

I turned to Thang. "Get Jean Pierre up here, our Chief Engineer, I told you once before he's the nearest we have to a doctor. These people need some help."

Thang stared at me curiously, slightly bewildered.

"You would help to save the lives of Viet Cong?"

"Damn your politics," I said harshly. "I can only see dying men. Jean Pierre may not be able to do much, but he'll do what he can."

"Your western way of thinking is strange," Thang pointed out. "You cannot watch an individual suffer pain before your eyes, and yet you willingly permit American planes to drop napalm on Vietnamese villages to destroy the whole population. Do you not realize that villages are made up of individuals, and that napalm causes much individual death and suffering?"

"I'm not American," I told him. "I'm British." But then I grabbed the shoulder of his borrowed robe and pointed down at Evelyn Ryan. "But she's American— and she's down there on her knees tying bandages on to one of your damnfool guerilla fighters."

Thang removed my hand uncertainly from his shoulder. He looked too baffled to be offended.

"I will send for the Chief Engineer," he promised. And then he went out.

Evelyn looked up at me and tried to explain:

"The Vietnamese can face pain. They can accept death and suffering as part of a familiar pattern. They can be cruel too, and they quite happily torture prisoners. But they don't deal in overkill, and magadeath and

132

chemical warfare, and technological genocide. It's just a different way of thinking."

She bowed her head over her patient again, a thin boy with a smashed leg, and Howard Deakin knelt down beside her as they continued their work.

I moved round to the Captain. Butcher was awake and he turned his head to look at me with strained eyes.

"That was a hell of a way you parked my ship, Mister Steele!"

"I'm sorry, sir. I had to come in fast and blind. It wasn't exactly under normal conditions."

"I know. What's the damage?"

I recounted the list and his mouth tightened and his fist clenched.

"Damn them—and damn this stupid leg!" He winced as he tried to move the splinted limb, and then he looked at me again. "I'm not blaming you, Johnny. I would have been forced to do the same."

I nodded and asked: "Where's Ching?"

"In his cabin. Mrs Deakin patched him up and then he wanted to return to the foredeck. I had to order him to stay below. He would have been a liability on deck, and I reckoned that you and the Bo'sun could handle things there. Besides—" He gave me a searching look. "You'll have to stop and sleep soon, Johnny. You look as though you've been hauled through a typhoon."

"I can manage," I said. "There's a few hours in me yet."

"I don't doubt it, but don't burn yourself out before it's necessary. It's my guess that they'll want to sail again as soon as possible, but the Third Officer is resting and he can give you a break as soon as we clear the island. And use the Bo'sun, Johnny. He's a reliable man. Let him stand a watch on the open sea."

"I'll do that," I answered. "But right now I want to check our hull where we bashed into the harbour wall. I don't want to clear Hon San and then find that we've sprung a leak."

I saluted him and he acknowledged weakly, and then I went out.

133

One of Thang's guards followed me at a respectful distance but made no attempt to interfere with my movements. I returned to the foredeck and conferred with Ho Wan, and we left the ship and went down on to the harbour wall to inspect the damage. Dinh joined my guard and followed us without comment.

The Viet Cong had fixed up a couple of rough planks to act as an improvised gangway, and already they were bringing the released prisoners aboard. They made a straggling column of rake-thin wretches who varied from the frankly joyful to the dumb creatures who still stumbled in a daze, and Ho Wan and I had to wait for a gap in the line before we could descend.

Behind the *Shantung* the five big junks were moored and they too were absorbing smaller columns of the ex-prisoners. The whole operation was being conducted with great haste and much shouting, for even now an American air strike could sink us all. Along the harbour the wooden buildings, probably the administration blocks, and at the far end the radio station, had all burned out into heaps of ash and blackened timbers, and the corpses of the defenders scattered the island like obscene confeitti.

A sharp explosion made us turn our heads to look across the small bay, now blue and sparkling in the morning sunlight. The last of the three big 155 millimetre guns on the south side of the harbour mouth had been demolished by experts and we watched it tilt over and slide into the sea.

"They forget nothing," Ho Wan observed sombrely.

I nodded and we walked forward beneath the bows. Here the whole of the dockside was ruptured and crushed inwards, the planks and timbers snapped and twisted and jutting into the air like half-chewed bones. We approached carefully and Wan squatted down to gaze at the badly dented plates in the ship's hull. In one place the rusted bolts had snapped clean and the steel had gaped open like a wound torn along a dotted line. Fortunately the heavy damage was the height of the harbour wall, a good ten feet above sea level.

"Not good," was Ho Wan's comment.

"Bad enough," I agreed. "But we can patch it. We'll have to strengthen those plates from inside."

"I can fix," Wan said. "But how much time?"

We returned to where Dinh and my guard were standing on solid ground. He looked at me inquiringly and I asked:

"How soon do you expect this ship to sail?"

"As soon as everyone is aboard—an hour perhaps. There can be no delay, Chief Officer!"

"Then it will have to be a temporary job, and we'll all pray that we don't run into a storm. Let's go on with it, Bo'sun."

We started to return to the ship but I stopped when I saw Lin Chi coming down the crude gangway. Behind her was Huynh Quoc, picking his steps like a yellow-robed old woman crossing a busy road. Evelyn Ryan followed them, and then one of the monk guerillas. Lin Chi hurried towards me.

"Johnny, I have been looking for you."

"I've been busy," I said.

She looked uncertainly at Dinh and my guard, and then the old monk came up behind her. He placed his palms together and became their spokesman.

"Mister Steele, we have a request to make of you. We are going ashore to find Miss Lin Chi's father, and we ask you to please accompany us?"

I stared at him. "Why?"

"Because we wish you to see for yourself what conditions are like on this island. Miss Lin Chi wishes you to understand why we have to do these things. Will you come?"

I looked at Lin Chi, she too had her hands clasped together and looked very small and vulnerable. Her smooth face was pale and calm, but there was anguish in her eyes.

"Please, Johnny. I want you to understand."

I exchanged glances with Ho Wan and he tugged one side of his soot-streaked moustaches.

"I can do repair job. No worry."

Dinh said sharply: "Has Section Leader Thang approved?"

"Yes." Huynh Quoc nodded humbly. "And also he had given permission for Miss Ryan to come ashore. The Section Leader agrees that they should try to appreciate our motives."

Dinh shrugged. "Very well, but you must hurry. There is not much time." He spoke warningly to the two guards who were to act as our escort and then stood aside.

I was still hesitant. My first job was the safety of the ship and I didn't like to delegate that responsibility, but at the same time I had every confidence in Ho Wan and I couldn't deny the pleading in Lin Chi's eyes. I nodded and the Bo'sun preceded Dinh back to the ship.

"We must make haste," Huynh Quoc repeated, and he began to lead the way. Lin Chi kept pace beside him and I followed with Evelyn Ryan. The two guards brought up the rear.

We had to circle round the battered section of the harbour, and then followed the scattered lines of released prisoners back to their source. A narrow tarmac road led between the burned out buildings and the shell of the radio station, and beyond was a cleared valley between the low, jungle clad hills that made up the central bulk of the island. The Viet Cong regulars with their rifles and sub-machine guns slung were hurrying to and fro to hustle their liberated friends along, and were ignoring the dead guards sprawled in the dust. A few prison guards sat here and there by the roadside, prisoners in their turn with their hands clasped on top of their heads looking miserably into the muzzles of Viet Cong weapons.

Evelyn stumbled, her foot slipping on one of the hundreds of empty cartridge cases that were littered with the stink of cordite, and I reached out a hand to steady her. She looked worn out, and now there were darker stains of red on her dark shirt and jeans. Her eyes were red-rimmed with deep shadows.

"You shouldn't have come," I said.

"I didn't want to," she answered wryly. "I thought that I could be of more use on the ship. But then your Chief Engineer came up to the saloon and Howard and

Janet insisted that they could manage without me. They're two wonderful people, so quiet that you hardly notice them but they've been working non stop since the first casualties were brought in. Your steward has become devoted to Janet Deakin. I'm sure he thinks that she's some kind of a saint."

"Hong is a good judge of character," I said. "And once you win his loyalty he holds nothing back."

We had fallen a few yards behind Lin Chi and the old monk, and Evelyn indicated their backs with a gesture.

"They've been helping too, as much as they were able. They were with us in the saloon until just before you arrived. Both of them are terribly upset by all this killing and bloodshed, especially the old monk. That's why I felt that I had to come ashore when they asked me. It's important to them that they justify themselves, and somehow they seem to regard you and me as their judges. How crazy can you get?"

She stopped talking because we had reached the barbed wire gateway that led into the main compound of the prison camp, and our hosts had paused to wait for us to catch up. The double gates had been blasted wide open, either by a hand grenade or a mortar shell, and just inside were the smoking remains of an office building that had been burned to the ground. The twelve foot fence that encircled the camp was made up with stout wooden posts bedded in concrete and closely strung with the hideous strands of barbed wire, but the hand grenades had breached it in a dozen places where the ex-prisoners were pouring out to freedom. There had been one watch tower that had been decapitated and toppled beside its shattered wooden struts, and outside the camp to our left was a double row of wooden buildings which still blazed merrily. I guessed that they had provided staff accommodation, but now they were a basis for dancing flames and the clouds of black smoke that blotted out the jungle green of the hillside, and lifted up to stain the clear blue sky.

Inside the fenced compound was a wide exercise yard, and beyond a block of six long and very low concrete huts with corrugated roofing. From the huts the released prisoners still emerged in batches, hustled along by the armed guerillas, and Lin Chi stared towards them as she sought to identify her father. She was impatient but we all had to wait for the old monk.

Huynh Quoc had walked as though in a bad dream through all the dead and wounded South Vietnamese guards who had littered our path, and now there were two distorted corpses lying square across the demolished gateway into the camp. The old monk had his hands clasped and his face bowed towards them, and I saw that his eyes were tightly closed. His wrinkled face was white with grief. Lin Chi put out her hand as though to touch him and comfort him, but then she remembered that a woman must not touch a man who had taken the vows of the yellow robe. She withdrew her hand again and her face shared some of his pain.

I realized then that not only had they believed that the *Shantung* would be taken without bloodshed, they had also believed that Hon San could be invaded without bloodshed. Perhaps they had honestly believed that the high merit in their cause would shame away all opposition, and now they were shocked by the events they had set in motion.

One of our pseudo-monk guards spoke sharply from behind me, and I guessed that he was reminding them that we must not waste time. Lin Chi looked past me helplessly but Huynh Quoc remained transfixed. I stepped forward and touched his bony shoulder where it thrust from the folds of his robe.

"We came to find Lin Chi's father," I said gently.

He opened his eyes and they were mirrors of suffering. Then he nodded slowly and began to lead on, but his hands remained clasped in front of him and every knuckle was a white bone that threatened to burst through the tightened skin.

We crossed the open exercise yard, but now Huynh Quoc was walking in a kind of mechanical slow motion and the more forceful of our two guards lost patience and hurried ahead. The first two huts had already been cleared, but our guard made insistent inquires from the

138

freed prisoners and guerillas who were still hurrying past from the huts that remained, and finally we were directed to number five. The guard stood back and gestured us to go inside.

Lin Chi led the way apprehensively and the old monk followed. I came next with Evelyn just behind me and we all had to turn sideways to ease through the door against the stream of men coming out. I expected to see rows of bunk beds or even hard wooden benches, but this was nothing like the conventional prison camp. There was just a wide catwalk down the centre of the long hut, and on either side a line of small, square concrete pits. At the far end of the hut the pits were still covered by a grille of steel bars, but the gratings sealing the nearer pits had been removed and the men inside were either climbing or being lifted out. Each pit was perhaps five feet wide by ten feet long, and was totally isolated from its neighbours. They reeked of urine and excrement from the leaking barrels with which each pit was furnished, and there was nothing else except the metal rods whereby the prisoners had been shackled to the walls.

Huynh Quoc looked into my face, and this time he was not shocked because he had known what to expect. This time I was feeling shocked and horrified.

"They call them tiger cages," the old man said.

It was a good description, for the prisoners could have fared no better than caged animals.

"My God," Evelyn said slowly. She had shown more courage than any other woman I had ever known but now she looked sick. "I never knew it could be as bad as this!"

Lin Chi had hurried ahead along the catwalk to search for her father, but I hung back for a moment to take in the full scene. A large barrel leaking white powder stood by the catwalk and when I looked inside I realized that it contained lime. For a moment it seemed too barbaric to be possible, but there was shovel standing by the lime barrel and its presence here could have only one explanation. Lime burned, and a shovelful thrown down through the iron bars on to the heads of

139

the trapped and half naked men in the cages would quieten even the most defiant spirits of resistance.

I was still trying to believe it all when I heard Lin Chi cry out, and I looked up to see her kneeling at the far end of the catwalk with her face pressed close to the grating of one of the sealed pits. She was sobbing and speaking incoherently in Vietnamese, but then she looked back and called my name.

"Johnny! Please, Johnny!"

I hurried towards her with Evelyn at my heels, ignoring the baffled stares we received as we pushed our way through. The Vietnamese girl was struggling to lift up the heavy grille when we reached her and I took it from her hands and heaved it to one side. Below were three emaciated Asian faces, all desperately trying to help themselves and clamber out, while in one corner of the cage an old man simply knelt in open-eyed prayer. Lin Chi scrambled down into the pit and threw her arms around him, and then his eyes closed as they wept and embraced each other.

I helped to haul two of the younger men out, but the third who wore the tattered rags of a yellow robe stayed to help the old man and the girl. I jumped down beside them, and then waited awkwardly until Lin Chi had recovered from the first emotion of her reunion.

"This is my father," she said at last. "His name is Tho Lin Vien." Her voice faltered too much for her to introduce me in turn, but that could wait.

"Let's get him out," I said softly.

Lin Vien opened his eyes and focused them upon my face. There were tears running down his sunken cheeks as he still clung to his daughter, but he controlled himself so that neither his tears nor his rags nor his unkempt appearance could affect his dignity.

"I am sorry," he apologized, and it was obvious that he had not spoken English for a long time. "But my legs are paralysed. I cannot walk."

"I can carry you," I said.

He smiled at that and croaked wryly:

"You will not find me heavy. They do not fatten us here. We receive just a little fish and rice, although sometimes we can catch beetles or a lizard in order to stay alive. My companions have been good friends, because I am the weakest they save for me the best pieces."

I waited until Lin Chi reluctantly broke their embrace to give me room and then lifted the old man up on to the catwalk. He was weak and thin and could not have weighed any more than seventy pounds. The young priest who had been his cell mate watched anxiously but I did not need his help, and in fact I had to help him out in turn.

I spent the next five minutes in angrily hurling aside the rest of the iron gratings and drawing up more pitiful wretches from their living death inside the tiger cages. Some were priests and some were not, perhaps some were hardcore Communists murderers but I didn't care. My two guards must have felt the same for they slung their combat rifles and worked beside me. For the moment we had no quarrel.

When all of the concrete pits were empty I returned to Lin Vien and knelt to lift him again. He delayed me a moment while he threw a small scrap of cloth into his empty cage, and watched it settle on the floor before meeting my eyes.

"They did not find it necessary to give us toilet paper," he said. "So for the past six months I have used that small piece of my shirt, and each time that I have used it I have washed it out with my urine so that I could use it again. For all of us it was the only way to stay clean, but I am glad that at last I can throw my toilet cloth away."

He made the admission quietly, and the fact that I found incredible was that he could make it with dignity. I had no words to answer him, and I could only lift him as reverently as possible and carry him back to the ship.

CHAPTER FOURTEEN

I BROUGHT the *Shantung* safely out of Hon San harbour an hour later and set her bows for the open sea. Behind us the island lay still and silent under a wide pall of spreading smoke. The activity was over for all of the prisoners had been carried away, and the survivors of the South Vietnamese guards had been bundled into captivity and left locked in their own tiger cages, a taste of their own medicine with which I could find no quarrel. They would only have to endure for a few hours what their ex-charges had endured for years.

The fleet of Viet Cong junks had already sailed, laden almost to the point of sinking with their human cargoes, and were dispersing to all points of the horizon as they ran for cover. If that blanket of black smoke that covered Hon San climbed any higher it would soon be visible for a score of miles, and must inevitably attract the attention of any patrolling US plane. The junk skippers knew that they had to depart with all speed.

From my position on the bridge I looked down on our own cluttered decks, which were now almost hidden under a seething mass of political refugees. For them the *Shantung* had become a ferry to hope, and now that I had seen the tiger cages I was prepared to relent and sail them to sanctuary, but at the same time I had grave doubts on the *Shantung*'s chances. We were going to be the obvious target when the angry US Air Force came hunting for its prey, and unlike the junks we had no hope of masquerading as a simple fishing vessel.

Thang and Dinh stood on the bridge behind me, and once we had cleared the island I turned to face them. I had not forgotten Ralph Yorke and David Kee, and I still intended to kill Section Leader Thang at the first real opportunity, but that was a personal thing now. It would have to wait because the future of the refugees now ranked with the safety of my ship as priority.

"What course?" I demanded.

Thang said calmly: "Set the course for Cambodia. Our destination is the neutral port of Sihanoukville."

"I had expected North Vietnam?"

"That is too far away, Chief Officer. Sihanoukville is within thirty hours sailing time, even for this ship, and also we do not wish to force an issue with the American Air Force. I do not think that they will sink a British ship with American hostages, especially if we aim for a neutral port. They may act like murderers inside Vietnam, but they have no wish to be recognized as such by the world."

"You're going to cause one hell of a political crisis with the Cambodians."

Thang shrugged carelessly. "When there is a war no nation has the right to expect peace and neutrality. War decides whose might is right. War creates empires and only fools believe that fighting brings peace. I am a soldier and I despise pacifists and neutralists." He looked down on to our decks and his lip twisted scornfully. "There are many here whom I would willingly have left behind. They are of no more use to the Communist empire than they are to the American empire."

I remembered Shakespeare, *What's in a name?*, and decided not to argue with him on his definition of terms. Empire, Power-bloc, Sphere of Influence—perhaps it did all boil down to the same basic level.

I turned away to the chart room and plotted out the new course for Cambodia.

I stayed on the bridge until Hon San had vanished behind the receding horizon, and the *Shantung* was alone again between the double blue vastness of the sea and sky. The ship was steady on her new course with the engines full ahead and so I went forward to inspect our damaged bows. Ho Wan had completed the task of closing the gap between our buckled plates, and the whole bulkhead was now solidly braced from inside. I checked his work only because it was my responsibility and my job, I knew that I would find no fault.

When we returned to the deck the Bo'sun dismissed the crewmen who had helped him with the repairs, and then he looked at me inquiringly. He had worked hard through a busy morning but he was not yet bone-weary as I was.

"Wan," I asked him, "can you stand a watch on the bridge until noon? I want to be sure that I'm alert if anything else happens, and our Third Officer is still recovering from that crack over the eye."

Wan smiled bleakly and touched the grimy dressing that still adorned his own check.

"All same now. Very fashionable." And then more formally: "Yes, Mister Steele, I can stand the watch. I call you if needed. Until then you sleep."

I thanked him and then we ascended to the bridge. Thang listened to my decision and made no objections. His mission was accomplished and he knew that there was no longer any point in our attempting to reclaim our ship. With such an excess of pro-Viet Cong passengers it would also have been impossible.

I gave the Bo'sun the course and then left him to hold the ship steady. We were sailing west southwest and it would be several hours before we passed the southern tip of Vietnam and would need to turn north. If we could turn that corner then perhaps we could even consider ourselves safe from interception, but I doubted it.

I went down to the saloon to make a report to the Captain before seeking my bunk, and found it even more over-crowded than before. Howard and Janet Deakin still toiled slowly among the wounded and the sick and half starved refugees who needed medical attention, and Huynh Quoc was now working with them. Jean Pierre had returned to his engine room to nurse the *Shantung* out of Hon San, and my last request of him had been that he too should hand over to his second in command and try to get some sleep.

Howard stood up as I entered. His face had a pasty yellow look and he swayed a little, as though he might be due for a bout of fever. He acknowledged me with a nod and took off his spectacles to clean them.

"Where are the two girls?" I asked.

"Lin Chi is with her father," he said quietly. "And I sent Evelyn to her own cabin to rest. She was very tired."

"We're all tired," I said wryly, and gave him a searching look. "You're tired too, and so is Janet. If you don't ease up soon then both of you will collapse."

"We have to help these people as much as we can, for as long as we can." He spoke without doubt and then smiled faintly. "Do not worry about us, Mister Steele. Janet and I are no strangers to all this, and we know our limitations. When we can do no more, that is the time to stop and rebuild our own strength."

"Was it really as bad as this in Vietnam?"

"Sometimes. I have seen our mission hospital almost as crowded." His voice became heavy with sadness. "Their hurts were always the same, cholera, dysentery, malaria, and of course the endless war damage."

He became silent and I stared at him, for he surpassed my understanding. He replaced his spectacles and looked round vaguely for his next patient.

"Howard," I said slowly. "You told me once that you had failed with your time in Vietnam!"

He hesitated and gazed at me blankly. Then he remembered and nodded.

I moved my hand to indicate all the helpless human flotsam around us that he had bandaged and tended to the best of his ability.

"After what you've done for all these poor devils can you still say that? If in Vietnam you could only relieve a tenth of the suffering that you've relieved here—how can you possibly say that you have failed?"

He was still hesitant, as though he didn't quite understand my question, but then he tried to explain:

"Mister Steele, my wife and I were trained as preachers, as missionaries, not as doctors. Our task was to spread the knowledge of Our Lord Jesus Christ, to

145

bring light into the souls of men who needed Him. Of course we have tried our best to perform a task for which we were not prepared, we had no alternative, but we are servants of the Catholic Church, and in our real task, the task of saving men's souls, we have failed!"

I wanted to shake him, but gently. It was a peculiar paradox of feeling.

"Howard," I said patiently. "Can you really measure your success only in converts? In the work you've done and the way you've lived you have followed the *example* of your Lord Jesus Christ! You've practised compassion and you only have to look at the faces of the poor wretches you've helped to know that they're grateful. Does it really matter that you haven't taught them His name? Or that you haven't converted them to the Catholic Church. Surely just by spreading compassion you've achieved all that any man can?"

"Perhaps—" He looked bewildered. "I hadn't thought of it in that light."

"Then think of it now."

He nodded and swayed unsteadily, and I had to step forward and catch him. Janet and Hong were suddenly hovering anxiously at my side, and I relinquished him to their charge.

"Take him down to your cabin," I told his wife. "And both of you stay there and sleep for at least a couple of hours before you try to do any more. That's an order."

Janet was too tired to argue, and with the steward fussing to clear their way they slowly left the saloon. Huynh Quoc looked up from the patient he was tending to watch them depart and I saw that he was equally fatigued, also he was an older man, but I suspected that he had set himself a heavy penance for his sins and so I did not interfere. He bowed his head to his work and I turned to the Captain.

Butcher was conscious and had been listening. He smiled at me faintly.

"Preaching to a preacher, that's a new job for you, Johnny. I didn't know you were a religious man."

146

"I'm not sure that I am," I said. "But at least I'm a thinking man, and some things do seem obvious."

He chuckled but it turned into a cough. "How many years have we sailed together, Johnny? It must be quite a few. And I still don't know how or what you think. Does that make me a failure as a Captain?"

"I don't think so, sir. I've been learning a lot myself in the past thirty-six hours."

I sat down at the table and began to give him my report, and as I talked I became gradually aware of the foul smell, like rotting fruit or rotting flesh. I glanced round to discover which one of the sick or wounded Vietnamese was responsible, and Butcher said wryly:

"You don't have to be polite, Johnny. I know that it's me."

I stared at him, and his grey eyes were dull but calm under the gold braided peak of his cap. Slowly I turned my head and looked down at his splinted leg. The smell was stronger and now I could identify it.

"Gangrene?"

He nodded weakly. "Old Frog didn't want to tell me, and neither did our missionary friends. But I know."

"We should reach port in thirty hours." I tried to match his calmness. "Less if Jean Pierre knows that we need all the steam he can get. There must be a hospital at Sihanoukville, or at least at Phnom Penh."

"And save this fat useless lump at the expense of my leg." He slapped his body and grimaced. "I'm not sure that I want that, Johnny."

There was nothing that I could say, and I realized later that my fist had tightened and crushed my regulation cap. Butcher saw and closed the conversation for me.

"Go to your bunk, Mister Steele. Turn in and get some sleep. And that's another order."

I must have slept for about three hours before I was rudely awakened. I heard the door open but Assistant Section Leader Dinh was urgently shaking my shoulder even before I could open my eyes. His usually noncha-

147

lant grin was missing and his flat, yellow face was stiff and serious under his coolie hat.

"You must come on deck, Chief Officer. The American warplanes are coming!"

I grabbed my cap, the only article of clothing I had bothered to remove, and followed him out at a run. We hurried briskly to the foredeck, and there I saw that the Viet Cong regulars and the refugees from Hon San had all been cleared away from the foreward cargo hatch. The Deakins and Evelyn Ryan had been brought up to stand in lonely isolation on the raised hatch cover, and their faces showed uncertainty and perhaps a little fear, and resignation to their fate.

I looked up and saw three jet trails criss-crossing the clear blue sky. They were white streaks of vapour drawn by black pencil points that were three F-4 Phantoms coming back to take their second curious look.

Lin Chi came to meet me and explain, and her eyes were unhappy and confused.

"Johnny, you must stand on the hatch cover with the Americans. The American pilots in the aeroplanes will not drop their bombs if they see that we have non-Asian people aboard."

"I hope you're right," I said.

I glanced up to the bridge and saw Thang looking down on me, and beside him the larger and even more piratical figure of Ho Wan. The Bo'sun leaned forward and called clearly:

"What orders, Mister Steele?"

I hesitated a second, and then shrugged my shoulders.

"Hold your course, Bo'sun. If they do play rough we're a sitting duck anyway."

I stepped up on to the cargo hatch and Evelyn Ryan gave me her hand.

"Welcome to our stage," she said. "I'm not sure whether we're just on display, or whether we're expected to perform."

I answered her smile and then the first of the Phantoms came streaking overhead with a thunderous roar. I stretched my neck upwards and saw that the plane was

148

tilted on to one wing, and there was a brief glimpse of two puzzled faces staring down at us from the streamlined cockpit. The jet buzzed our bows within spitting distance of the bridge but not a shot was fired. The gun teams had been prudently withdrawn from the two twenty-five pounders in our bows, and the machine guns on the bridge had been carefully left unmanned with their barrels pointing harmlessly at our own decks. Everyone could see the sleek missiles tucked against the underbelly of the Phantom, and there were two more covering their flight-mate from above and a whole Air Force on call. It was obvious that nobody on the *Shantung* was going to fire the first shot to invite a battle.

The Phantom zoomed away, giving us a rude, red view of its flaming backside, and once it had regained a comfortable altitude number two peeled off into a dive. Each jet in turn screamed across our bows, coming closer each time, and I realized that they were trying to turn us aside and back towards Vietnam. I looked up to the bridge but Thang and Ho Wan were standing rigid. I had told the Bo'sun to maintain his course and he would do just that, and Thang would never give an order that would accept defeat.

Lin Chi was standing with her hands pressed over her ears, and after the third Phantom had dived and they all showed unmistakable signs of coming back again she scrambled up on to the hatch beside me.

"Johnny, what are they trying to do?"

I said wryly: "No doubt they've tried to make radio contact with us and they've failed, because we haven't any radio. They can see from our armament and all the people on board that we must have been involved in the raid on Hon San, and this is their way of telling us that they want us to return to Saigon."

"We will not return," she said defiantly. But then she pressed into my arms and buried her face against my chest as the leading Phantom howled close over our heads.

For the next ten minutes they buzzed us continually until I felt that my eardrums must be shattered beyond repair. Howard knelt and wrapped his arms around Janet's head in a vain effort to protect her from the deafening sound, and Evelyn kept close to myself and Lin Chi. All of our refugee passengers had fled to the stern of the ship, and only Dinh and three of the original monk guards remained on the foredeck. On the bridge Thang and Ho Wan stolidly ignored the reckless antics of the jet pilots.

The Phantom leader made one final attempt, aiming straight for the bridge and hurtling down as though he had fully accepted the idea of suicide. Lin Chi screamed and even Evelyn pressed close enough for me to encircle her with my free arm, but I knew, or at least prayed, that that oncoming jet jockey didn't really have a *kamikaze* mind. I gave no orders and the Bo'sun stood fast on the bridge. The Phantom lifted up only seconds before he would have crashed and the thunder of his passing was an agony with the heat of his exhaust scorching the deck.

It was the last attempt to turn us, and after circling high for a few more minutes the three jets gave a rolling shrug of their wings and departed for the eastern horizon.

"You see," Lin Chi said weakly. "They are not prepared to drop their bombs and sink us, and so they can do nothing."

I didn't answer her for I hadn't the heart to tell her that the Phantoms were only forward observers, and that next to arrive on the scene there would almost certainly be a US Navy patrol boat with orders to stop and board the *Shantung*. Their ferry of hope was in reality a ferry without hope, and I didn't like to think of what would happen then.

Thang was also aware that his enemies would not give up so easily, and so he kept us all sitting on the hatch cover under guard throughout the long afternoon. I asserted myself just sufficiently to change the watch on the bridge, relieving the Bo'sun and replacing him with Ching who emerged from his cabin capable and refreshed. Ho Wan chose to join me on the foredeck with our passengers and was content to stretch out and sleep there in the sun.

There was nothing that any of us could do except talk or doze. The Deakins fretted because they had been parted from the people who needed them, while Evelyn simply sat and watched the horizon. There was no shade on the open deck and Lin Chi stayed just to share our broiling ordeal. No doubt she was feeling guilty, for she kept repeating her regret that it was necessary for us to remain here in the fierce heat.

It was late afternoon when the next interruption came. Ho Wan heard it as soon as I did and we stood up together. The Bo'sun had brought a pair of binoculars down from the bridge, and he focused them briefly off our starboard bow and then handed them to me without comment. His face was grave.

I sighted the glasses, even though I already knew that my earlier anticipation had been wrong and our new visitor was no patrol boat. It was not a boat at all, but a gaggle of black spots in the horizon sky. They were too slow and dumpy to be Phantoms, but they were lethal none the less. I picked out the lead plane and recognized the more old-fashioned shape of a Skyraider. It was American-built but the wings and fuselage carried the more ominous markings of the South Vietnamese Air Force.

There were a dozen aircraft in the flight and they wasted no time in examining the ship for hostages. They were less handicapped by scruples than the American pilots, and no doubt they had more reason for ensuring that a ship-load of escaped Communists did not get away. If they knew that there were hostages aboard then they would apologize afterwards and blandly pretend that they had acted in ignorance. It was only necessary to maintain the right face to the world.

The Skyraiders dipped their wings and came straight in to the attack.

CHAPTER FIFTEEN

I GRABBED up the two girls and yelled to Ho Wan, but the Bo'sun had already predicted my order. He gathered up the terrified Janet Deakin in one arm, and clamping his free hand on Howard's shoulder he ran them both off the foredeck and into the mouth of the port alley leading to the stern of the ship. I hustled Evelyn and Lin Chi to the same sanctuary and practically threw them the last part of the way before diving in on top of their sprawling bodies. Dinh shouted from behind me but his three guards were also scattering and then the Skyraiders were upon us.

They swept down with cannon blazing and shells raked the whole ship from stem to stern. The *Shantung* jerked and writhed in helpless agony and the hideous sound of mass screaming was the only thing that could drown the thunder of repeated explosions. Metal ripped and timbers tore and the crackle of flames began to add to the sound, and then black smoke started to wreathe its way through the ship. The Skyraiders continued to attack and their sole aim was to hammer us to the bottom of the sea.

I got to my knees and hauled both girls closer in against the superstructure. While the shells struck from the starboard side we were relatively safe, but if they wheeled and attacked from the port flank we had no protection at all. Both girls were white and Lin Chi was sobbing.

"They are trying to kill us all," she said. "We did not think that the Americans would do that."

"They're not Americans," I shouted savagely. "They're South Vietnamese planes."

152

"They should not try to kill us," she repeated stubbornly.

"Now that we are sailing away from Vietnam why can't they let us go?"

"But they *are* trying to kill us!" I cursed her. "Damn you and your blind stupidity! You've saved your people only to destroy them."

My anger sparked off a flash of spirit inside her and she cried hysterically:

"At least we are no worse than the Americans who destroy our people first while they pretend to save them!"

It was the wrong moment to argue for we could barely hear ourselves speak above the crash of the explosions and the sounds of the carnage that was being wrought above decks. Ho Wan was looking to me for orders with Janet Deakin still held fast in his arms, and Howard crouched beside him.

"Get them all down to the saloon," I said grimly. "It's as safe as anywhere." His eyes lifted upwards and I added. "I'll attend to the bridge. You just keep these people together. Be ready to get them all up to the boats when we get the chance."

"Aye, aye, Mister Steele."

He nodded and I pushed Evelyn and Lin Chi towards him and left him to it. James Ching was on the bridge and I couldn't leave the Third up there alone to hold down my responsibility.

I ducked out on to the foredeck again and swung rapidly up the nearest companionway. There was no sign of Dinh although his three friends sprawled dead around the burning cargo hatch, and I was only vaguely aware that the two Viet Cong gun teams had run to man their field pieces. The bridge itself was dancing with flames and when I reached it only two men were left standing in the wheelhouse. The helmsman and the seaman by the telegraph were both dead, and Ching himself was standing at the wheel. Thang had run out to the starboard machine gun and was crouching behind it.

The flock of Skyraiders had completed their first run and were turning for their second attack. Behind the bridge the boat deck and the lower decks beyond were a bloody slaughterhouse where cold blooded murder had been done amongst the close packed refugees. The *Shantung* was listing to port and burning in a score of places, but the Skyraiders were prepared to show no mercy. I watched them coming back, sweeping low over the sea, and then said tightly:

"Hard to port, Mister Ching."

Ching spun the wheel, the *Shantung* heaved slowly to port, and the first Skyraider, loosed its wing rockets and cannon into the sea off our starboard bow. Thang opened up with the machine gun and blazed away madly without doing any noticeable damage and the squat little fighter plane zoomed away unharmed. However, the rest of his squadron had time to shift their wings and compensate for our course change and they didn't miss.

The two gun teams crouched behind their twenty-five pounders in our bows and they each got off one shell. They fired them straight into the whirling nose props of the oncoming Skyraiders but the planes were approaching so fast that neither scored a hit. It was a vain, heroic and suicidal attempt. The planes were more accurate and concentrated all their cannon upon our bows. Within seconds the gun teams were mangled martyrs, blasted with their two-ton toy-pieces into the sea.

Thang was still operating the starboard machine gun, and on the port wing the two-man gun team had rallied to join him in putting up a show. Scattered combat rifles and submachine guns clamoured angrily from our decks, but they were only the grasped straws of dying men. The third Skyraider in line peeled off to concentrate on the port wing of the bridge and cut it away completely with a pin-pointed stream of cannon shells. The machine gun and the two gunners simply vanished as though they and the part of the bridge that supported them had been sliced off with a giant razor.

"Hard to starboard, Mister Ching."

I had to bellow to make myself heard and Ching spun the wheel again. I saw then that he was struggling and that there was blood soaking his right sleeve. He had been hit before I arrived but had said no word. I ran to help him and from the corner of my eye I saw another Skyraider streaking in to plaster the wheelhouse.

I didn't pause in my stride, but instead of reaching for the wheel I grabbed Ching himself by the shoulders and pulled him away. He stumbled and we fell together through the charthouse door. The shells smashed down behind us and the heat of the flames seared our faces. My ears were deafened and the bridge was an instant inferno with the roof of the wheelhouse crashing around our heels.

Ching was gasping in agony, the pain in his arm was suddenly stabbing through his whole nervous system and he was helpless. I dragged him further under the chartroom table and saw that there was a jagged splinter of shrapnel embedded just above his right elbow. The Skyraiders still pounded the wallowing *Shantung*, and even though I could not hear them I knew that the doomed wretches we had carried away from Hon San were still shrieking their death cries.

I looked back through the flames on the bridge, and saw that for the moment the sky ahead was clear. The Skyraiders were circling. I shouted to Ching:

"We have to get below. There's nothing we can do here!"

I couldn't hear my own words and neither could he, but he understood the movement of my lips and nodded weakly. I got him up to his feet and we ran together through the choking tongues of smoke and fire to reach the starboard wing of the bridge. I noticed that the surviving machine gun was now unattended but whether Thang had escaped alive or been toppled over the side dead I could not tell. I looked skywards and saw the first of the Skyraiders coming back like airborne hyenas to savage a kill.

I slithered down rapidly to the boatdeck without touching a single rung on the companionway, and then I turned to catch Ching as he tumbled down in my wake. There was not even a rifle firing from the *Shantung* now, but the Skyraiders were determined to massacre everything that moved. They had exhausted their cannon and rockets but the lead plane howled straight for Ching and myself with its machine guns spitting fire.

The boatdeck was already a shambles of blood and corpses and the mouth of the companionway to the deck below was half blocked by those who had tried to get away and failed. In the horror of the moment I had to kick a dead man aside before I could jump down and I yanked Ching bodily behind me. The Skyraider stitched rows of tracer across the deck boards behind us and all but clipped off the smokestack with one wing as it swept overhead. I landed hard on the deck below where more flames were raging and Ching thumped heavily on top of me.

For a moment I was winded, and I choked as I tried to suck the cordite and smoke laden air into my lungs. Then I succeeded in rolling Ching off my back and wriggling free. The young Chinese lay as though dead beside me, and I turned him over fearing to see a row of red holes across his shoulders. However I had dragged him down only just in time and mercifully he had only fainted from the pain of the fall. I hauled him in against a bulkhead and crouched over him until the last of the Skyraiders had emptied the tracer belts in its machine guns and turned away.

It was dusk and the *Shantung* was a blazing torch pouring a giant column of flames and oily black smoke into the darkening sky. The engines had stopped and I could feel the ship listing and slowly sinking. The Skyraiders had done their work well and even if they had not spent all their ammunition there would have been little point in them spending any more. They could afford to fly away and leave us to our fate and the sea.

My hearing was beginning to return and above the roar and crackle of burning I could hear wild animal cries coming from the boatdeck above. A new nightmare had begun and I realized that the living were fighting like wild beasts for places in the lifeboats.

I stood up and got Ching over one shoulder, and then began to run clumsily towards the saloon. Along the starboard alley a wall of fire forced me back and I had to retrace my steps and cross the ship to use the port side. Frantic men pushed past me, the refugees or Viet Cong regulars who had been lucky enough to be below decks when the air attack started. Some of them were wounded, blood-streaked or burned and soiled by smoke and terror. They were running for the upper decks or throwing themselves desperately into the flame-lit sea.

I reached the saloon and burst inside, and there I had to come to an immediate stop. The fire had not reached this part of the ship, but there was danger here and more death in the air. Ho Wan must have succumbed to Lin Chi's entreaties to save her father, for he had brought the old man up from her cabin and stood in the centre of the saloon with Lin Vien still cradled in his arms. Lin Chi stood beside him with her face full of anguish, and behind them Howard Deakin and Huynh Quoc stood hesitantly at either end of a stretcher that now bore the Captain. Evelyn Ryan stood beside them. Facing the party was our eternal enemy, Section Leader Thang, with two yellow-robed psuedo monks from his original unit. The three Viet Cong all held levelled combat rifles.

I had startled them all, but Thang's combat rifle whipped round to cover me. He was streaked with soot and his eyebrows had been scorched away, but otherwise he was unharmed and as ugly as ever. He stared at me and slowly I lowered Ching to the deck and then took another step forward. Ho Wan took advantage of the same pause to put down Lin Vien and motion Lin Chi gently aside. The Bo'sun's face was bleak and his eyes were lethal and I was glad that he was my friend and not my enemy.

I said harshly: "What the hell is going on here?"

"Chief Officer," Thang smiled at me savagely. "I thought that you were dead. I have ordered your man to lower a lifeboat for myself and my comrades, but he is foolish enough to refuse. He insists that all these useless people must also be saved."

"The Bo'sun is quite right." I would have shot Wan a

157

look of gratitude, but I did not dare to take my eyes away from Thang's. "We'll lower a boat for you—but these people all get places!"

"No!" Thang screamed the word violently and his face was contorted. "There will not be room for every-body. You will save my unit, and the men from the Hon San refugees whom I will select. We want only the peo-ple who will be useful to the National Liberation Front. The others must be left behind!"

This was the end, the final confrontation that had been written in our stars since Ralph Yorke and David Kee had died. There was no room for compromise now. One of us had to die and the combat rifle was in his hands. There was fear in my heart and ice in my brain, and with an effort of will the ice cooled the fear. I took another positive step forward.

"If you need me to lower a boat then you have to take these people along. It's as simple as that."

"Then die, Chief Officer!"

He lifted the combat rifle and the door burst open and Jean Pierre reeled in. For a split second Thang's gaze defected and I jumped him. Even then I would have died before I got past the combat rifle and it was a combination of factors that saved me. An automatic hand gun cracked loudly behind my right shoulder and there was a red hole just above and between Thang's hating eyes. I had him by the throat in almost the same moment, but I was holding a dead man.

The Bo'sun had matched me for speed and Thang's two men were slower than their leader. They had re-acted more instinctively to Jean Pierre's intrusion and swung to face the door. Ho Wan had the nearest guard in an instant, ripping the combat rifle from his hands and smashing the man away with a vengeful fist. The surviving guard dithered between three possible threats and before he could make up his mind who to shoot first I threw Thang at him and knocked him down. I grabbed up his rifle and used the butt to render him unconscious.

With the rifle in my hands and the Bo'sun also armed I had regained control of the saloon at least. There was time to pause and I looked round to see who had killed Thang. Evelyn Ryan stood behind me, her freckled face was pale but her hand was steady, and she was holding a .38 calibre automatic with a wisp of white smoke still dispersing from the barrel.

"You?" I said slowly.

She nodded and lowered the gun. Her hand began to tremble.

"But where did you get it?"

"It's part of my personal baggage. The American Central Intelligence Agency usually does issue its agents with arms." She looked at me helplessly. "John, you big lump, haven't you realized yet that that's why I had to snub you so rudely when you suggested that my cultural research project might be a cover for a branch of the CIA? Your joke was right on the mark. It *is* a CIA cover! My job was to keep watch on Lin Chi because we knew that she was the daughter of an important political prisoner—although I was told that Lin Vien was a diehard Communist."

I stared into those honey-brown eyes, which were suddenly distraught and appealing, and then I looked at the automatic again.

"That might have come in handy before. Why didn't you tell me that you had it tucked away in your stocking top, or wherever?"

"Because I haven't had it all the time. I collected it from my cabin on the night that the ship was hijacked, before I went up to the boatdeck to look for the lifeboat radio. Then Ghengis caught me by surprise and clobbered me and I lost the gun. I dropped it underneath one of the seats inside the lifeboat. I retrieved it last night when I sneaked that flare pistol, and fortunately Thang only spotted the flare pistol and not the thirty-eight. I've just kept it hidden and waited for the right chance to use it."

I smiled at her suddenly. "I won't complain," I said. "You couldn't have picked a better moment."

I turned my attention to Jean Pierre, who was already kneeling by the Captain. Our Chief Engineer had lost his cap and his white overall was soaked black with oil.

From his left shoulder streams of red mixed with the black mess and there was a ragged bullet wound just below his collar bone. He too had staggered in at exactly the right moment.

"What happened in the engine room?" I asked him.

"We rushed the guards on the catwalk," he said simply. "It was not so difficult because they were ready to break and run. My Third Engineer is dead, and I stopped one bullet. The rest of my crew have fled for the boats. but I came to find my Fat Friend."

"You should have gone with your crew, Old Frog," Butcher said weakly. "I'm not worth saving."

"I'll be the judge of that," I said. I looked to the Bo'sun. "Wan, you and I have to capture a lifeboat before those poor devils on deck wreck them all in their panic. Evelyn, you and Lin Chi can carry her father. He's not very heavy and Hong will help you. Howard—"

"Huynh Quoc and I can manage the Captain's stretcher," Howard assured me firmly.

Janet was helping Jean Pierre to stand, and the wounded Vietnamese patients were lifting up their friends who could not walk and waited hopefully. I looked for Ching and found that my Third Officer had recovered from his faint and regained his feet. With his left hand he had gathered up the last combat rifle from beside the fallen body of Thang.

"I am capable, Mister Steel," he said weakly.

"Mister Ching, you're a heroic liar. Lead the way behind us and bring all these people up to the boatdeck— and you have my permission to shoot anybody who tries to stop you."

He nodded and I knew that despite the fragment of shrapnel still wedged in his arm he would carry out my order. I had to leave them and go on ahead with the Bo'sun a formidable ally at my heels.

Outside the saloon the heat was intense. Parts of the *Shantung* were a white hot furnace and every alleyway was blind with smoke. We tried to press forward but were beaten back everywhere by the hungry flames. The ship was being gutted and timbers crashed and part of the decking along the port alleyway subsided in front

160

of us. It was impossible to reach the forward companionways to the upper decks, and we turned and retreated to the stern of the ship. We passed Ching and his struggling column and yelled at them to turn around and follow.

On the poop deck we burst out into the open air, although the flames and smoke still wreathed around us. The deck was strewn with corpses where the trapped refugees had been butchered like helpless cattle, and even the Bo'sun looked sick to his stomach. By the stern rail a small group of wounded and living knelt and prayed and among them were a scattering of yellow robes. Ho Wan automatically lifted his rifle but I knocked it down. They were not remnants of Thang's men but some of the priests who had been prisoners on Hon San. I recognized the young man who had shared Lin Vien's cell. These were the pacifists and neutralists, the people who did not want to kill, but preferred to draw themselves to one side and calmly wait for death.

"The boatdeck," I said grimly.

Ho Wan nodded and we ran up the ascending companionways together. As we gained the boatdeck we stopped and for a moment we were frozen with the horror of what was happening. Here the boards and the scuppers were littered twice as thick with the dead and dying, and it was as though the *Shantung* had literally sailed through a typhoon in a bloodbath. The distant bridge was a shambles of flames and another great gout of fire roared up from the smokestack where the steel plates glowed red. One of the port lifeboats had been pounded into splinters by the cannon shells of the Skyraiders but the other had been launched and was pulling strongly away from the ship. It was heavily overloaded and another score of heads bobbed desperately in the surrounding sea. In the bows I could see a little man with a coolie hat and I recognized Assistant Section Leader Dinh. He had survived and he knew how to operate a winch, and with that knowledge he had been able to launch a lifeboat.

On the starboard side the battle still raged amongst the survivors that were left. The forward lifeboat was still intact but the nearer boat was half cut free. They didn't know how to winch it down but someone had cut through the main rope securing the block and tackle to the stern. The lifeboat was hanging vertically and a man was standing on the bows, clinging to the remaining rope and endeavouring to hack it away with a heavy jungle knife at the same time. As we watched the rope parted and the lifeboat plummeted down stern first to hit the sea fifty feet below with an almighty crash. The man in the bows was slung away screaming with his knife still in his hand, and the lifeboat toppled to fall upside down. There had been more men hanging on desperately to the thwarts, but they were trapped and could only drown.

There were howls of dismay and some of the combatants automatically jumped or dived over the side. Others pushed each other aside to leap for the dangling lifelines and rapidly began slithering down. The score that remained rushed for the last lifeboat and began to battle for that. Among them there were still some of the Viet Cong regulars, including two of Thang's pseudo monks in their yellow robes. They all carried combat rifles and used them as clubs to restore order.

Perhaps they had already spent their magazines to cut the survivors to a manageable size, but the Bo'sun and I spared them no mercy. We sprinted forward, singled out the men who were still armed and opened fire. The false monks were our first target and we shot them dead. The remaining regulars turned and at least two of them were able to answer fire as the other survivors scattered and threw themselves flat in the scuppers. Bullets fanned the air beside my cheek, but I shifted my own combat rifle, selected my target and squeezed the trigger again. The Viet Cong spun away and vanished over the side, and the Bo'sun deftly shot his companion.

There had already been bitter fighting for places in the boats, much of it hand to hand, and the defeated wretches who were left were almost spent. The arrival of Ho Wan and myself with fresh arms and unused ammunition made them hesitate, and although they might not recognize Wan they could not fail to recognize the triple gold bars that still graced my shoulders. At the same time they were in fear of their lives and had already been driven to the point of madness. Their reaction was unpredictable and if they rushed us we could be swamped. I stepped forward and tried to get a sharp edge of authority into my voice.

"Stand fast there, all of you! If you let us get this boat launched properly then there'll be room for everybody."

I had to speak in English, it was the only language I knew, and apart from a small handful of our own Chinese seamen nobody understood. There were a score of wild-eyed, fear-crazed Vietnamese who began to move forward. They had spent God-knew-how-many years in the barbarous tiger cages of Hon San, and now they had been carried off on a hell ship that threatened to drown them in fire and blood. They had lost all sense of reason.

"Stand back!" I shouted above the roar of burning. I had my finger on the trigger and if they charged I would have to fire.

The Bo'sun was on my right flank and there was a sudden movement on my left. I half turned and saw that it was Ching who had run up to stand beside us. His rifle was almost useless with only one hand but at least it was a third rifle. The mob that faced us showed no sign of backing down and I was sick at heart as I realized that I would have to add to all the mess of murder that surrounded me.

Then there was another movement from behind, a patter of sandals and a yellow robe thrust between myself and the Bo'sun. Huynh Quoc stumbled forward and fell on to his knees with his hands outstretched and clasped together in prayer. He was blocking our line of fire and facing the mob around the lifeboat, and he began to speak shrilly and desperately in Vietnamese.

They could understand him and they were familiar with his robe, to them it meant more than my gold bars or the three rifles. They listened, and although one or two of them shouted back at him the old monk calmed them with his urgent words. I could only guess that he was translating what I had already tried to tell them, for they began to look to the Bo'sun and myself with hope instead of hatred.

I slung my rifle and looked round. The rest of the saloon party were struggling on to the boatdeck and Howard was standing by the Captain's stretcher where he and the old monk had set it down.

"The boat, Wan," I said curtly.

The Bo'sun slung his own rifle and we ran forward on either side of the kneeling Huynh Quoc. The mob parted tamely to let us through.

It was a matter of moments to tear away the life-boat's tarpaulin, and then to knock away the chocks and release the anchor chains. With the Bo'sun to lash them with orders our Chinese crewmen worked more efficiently to help and the boat was swiftly made ready to swing out. I turned then to Huynh Quoc, who was standing upright again with the flaming smokestack behind him, a humble old man who had somehow found the power to soothe the frightened creatures who clustered around him.

"Tell them to get aboard," I shouted. "And tell them to pack themselves in as tightly as they can. We'll save everybody if they don't panic."

He nodded and rapidly began to translate again. His words started a fresh scramble for the boat but at least it was a more orderly scramble. I turned to seek our own party and found that Evelyn and Lin Chi were close beside me, and that they were still struggling with the semi-paralysed Lin Vien. I took the old man from them and lifted him aboard, and then bundled both girls up behind him. Ching was standing back from the struggle, too near to fainting again to be of any practical help, but waiting as though he felt that it was his duty to let even our non-paying passengers board the lifeboat first. I had to order him to take his place. The Bo'sun helped him and I turned to Huynh Quoc.

"There's a whole group of your people down on the stern deck, they're just kneeling in a circle and praying. Bring them up here fast and I can save them."

He hesitated only a second and then he nodded

gratefully. He hoisted up his yellow robe around his knees and ran to give them the good news. The Bo'sun was busy heaving men bodily and unceremoniously into the lifeboat and I hurried back to where Howard and Janet Deakin still stood by the Captain's stretcher.

"What happened to Jean Pierre?" I demanded. I was sure that I had glimpsed him on deck when they had first appeared but now he had vanished.

The Deakins both looked distraught and it was Butcher who answered. He had already had some argument with Howard and he spoke firmly to me.

"Don't wait for Old Frog, Mister Steele. He isn't coming."

I stared down at him.

"What do you mean?"

"What I say. He isn't coming and neither am I." His voice was harsh but there was no harshness in his eyes. They were the eyes of a father regretting that he had to scold an over-protective son. He said more softly: "Take me to my bridge, Johnny. And if the wheel is still standing I want you to lash me to it."

"Don't be a fool," I said. "You're coming in the lifeboat."

"Johnny!" He reached up and gripped my wrist, and his hand had the strength of a vice. "Johnny, I'm an old man and I'm sick, and I've got gangrene stinking in my leg. I'm finished, Johnny, and so is Old Frog. He's got a smashed shoulder and he's too old to get another ship. This is *our* ship, the *Shantung* was our life—and if she's dying then the least that you can do is to let two useless old men die with her in our own way."

I knelt beside him and I felt that my mind and emotions were being torn apart.

"Where is Jean Pierre?"

"Gone back to his engine room, where else?" Butcher smiled as though he knew he had victory. "You're too late to stop him, Johnny. And you have no right to let him die alone."

"You can't listen to him," Howard shouted in my ear. He gripped my shoulder and shook me violently in his agitation. "Mister Steele, you can't listen to him!"

165

"Mister Steel, it's an order," Butcher spoke harshly again.

"It's the last one I shall ever give you. *Take me to my bridge!*"

I looked into his eyes and I understood, and I nodded slowly.

"Aye, aye, sir!"

I raised my head again and the Deakins were staring at me with horrified faces, both Howard and Janet.

"I'm sorry," I said. They couldn't understand, as I had just understood, how much a ship and the sea could mean to a man, and there was no time to explain. The cruellest thing I could do to Butcher would be to forcibly part him from his ship and his life-long friend, merely to become a crippled wreck washed up on the shore. I turned to the lifeboat.

"*Bo'sun!*"

Ho Wan came at a brisk run and I finished briefly:

"Give me a hand with the Captain's stretcher—we're taking him up to the bridge."

Wan stared at me, and then down at the Captain. Butcher gave him a faint smile and said in a quiet voice:

"Those are my orders, Bo'sun—and I'm still your Captain."

Wan continued to stare at him, but he was another man of the sea and he too understood. He bowed his head.

"Aye, aye, sir!"

We lifted the stretcher and I told Howard to waste no more time and get his wife aboard the lifeboat, and then we hurried to the bridge. The heat was fierce and it seemed that the whole superstructure was ablaze, and there was only one companionway that we could use on the port side. The starboard companionway was buckled out of shape and half of that wing of the bridge had already collapsed.

I went first, and with the Bo'sun holding the lower end of the stretcher at arm's length above his head we quickly carried Butcher aloft. The wheelhouse was gutted and the walls were gone, and only the wheel itself remained, charred and blackened but still standing. The chart room was on fire and more flames were licking up through the deckboards from the blaze below. We set the stretcher down by the wheel and there was a painful smile on Butcher's face.

"Help me up," he commanded. "Tie me to that wheel."

I threw his blanket aside and we lifted him upright. He braced himself on his right leg and leaned forward against the wheel, grasping the hot spokes with both hands.

"Tie me," he repeated, and there was sweat on his face.

Ho Wan was wearing an old scarf like a sash round his waist and he pulled it free. Quickly he passed it around Butcher's waist and through the spokes of the wheel. He knotted it with firm fingers, while I straightened the gold-braided cap that had started to slip sideways on Butcher's head. While we worked we suddenly felt the unmistakable thud of the engines starting up again deep in the bowels of the burning ship. We stopped and stared at Butcher who smiled again.

"Old Frog is back in his place," he said. "You can leave us now, Johnny. We'll take care of the *Shantung*."

I was still reluctant to turn away.

"If that's the way you really want it, sir?"

"This is the way I want it, Johnny!" The rough handling as we had moved him from his stretcher must have meant agony for his broken leg, for now the sweat was dripping from his jowls. "Your job is to get that lifeboat away. Be sure you get the decent people to safety."

"Aye, aye, sir."

The ship started to nudge forward and I realized that Jean Pierre must have put the engines to slow ahead. The *Shantung* was so low in the water that she barely moved.

"Go, Johnny," Butcher said hastily. "And you too, Bo'sun."

We nodded and turned away, but he remembered to add one final order:

167

"Johnny—when you get that boat launched stay clear of the other two boats that have got away. Do you understand?"

I didn't, but the order was plain enough, and so I acknowledged.

CHAPTER SIXTEEN

WE ran like hares for the lifeboat and found that everyone was now aboard, the yellow robes of Huynh Quoc and his priestly friends were quite distinctive. Altogether they made a tightly packed mass and the boat had been swung out ready for lowering with two of our Chinese sailors standing by each of the winch handles. Perhaps it would already have been lowered without waiting for Ho Wan and myself to return from our last errand to the bridge, except that Ching was standing in the stern with his AK–47 tucked threateningly under his sound arm. He wouldn't hit anything specific if he had to pull the trigger, but he would make a hell of a mess in the crowded lifeboat and so he had effective command.

The frightened, flame-lit yellow faces showed pure relief as they saw us racing back across the burning boatdeck, and without any further delay we took our places. The Bo'sun jumped into the stern while I boarded the bows. Ching had been right to wait for without us there was no one who could capably release the lifeboat once it hit the sea, and with the *Shantung* now forging slowly ahead that would be a tricky, split-second job if we were to get away from the hull without meeting disaster.

"Lower away!"

The four men on the winches obeyed my order, but one pair were more eager than the other. The lifeboat started to tilt and descend stern first and there were howls and screams from our frantic passengers.

"Lower together!" I roared. "Keep the boat level. Hold fast on that stern rope!"

The stern became steady for a moment and the bows dropped sharply.

"Hold fast!" I bellowed again. "Now together— Lower away!"

The boat started to descend again, rapidly but on an even keel. We dropped past the boatdeck and the deck below and I let the ropes pass up and down through my hands as I steadied myself in the bows with the tackle block at my feet. I turned my head briefly to check the stern but the Bo'sun had that end well under control. He had adopted my own position, standing upright and watching the approaching surface of the sea. I saw him glance round once while there was still time, and reach out a firm hand to press Ching down in his seat. We did not want our Third Officer to over balance and be lost at this stage.

We dropped below the last of the decks and began to descend past the rust-streaked hull. The gunwhales of the lifeboat scraped and bounced against the steel plates, and the movement became more violent as the ropes lengthened and we neared the sea. The *Shantung* was making barely a knot but it would be enough to turn the lifeboat over if we were dragged. The sea was close, a heaving swell that was rushing up fast. It was too late to shout any more orders for my voice would never have carried aloft, and I knew that the four sailors on the boatdeck had panicked and released the winch handles to run wild. I just prayed that neither of them would jam.

I crouched down with my hands on the tackle block, the rope still ripping through it, and then the lifeboat smashed down on a rising wave. The shock almost hurled me over the side but I was braced and as the boat lifted I unhooked the block and swung it away to crash against the ship's hull. There had been no time to look to Wan, I could only trust him, but his voice came precisely on cue with another ringing crash that echoed my own.

"Stern tackle block away, sir!"

There was no time for congratulations. The ship was pulling away and there were four sailors slithering frantically down the extended lifelines. I caught the nearest rope before it shipped away and let it pay out in a burning rush through my hands.

"Grab those lifelines!"

The Bo'sun was too far back but Howard and Evelyn Ryan were both swift to respond. Between us we held three of the lines just long enough to guide three men down into the boat. They fell heavily on top of us to create more confusion, while the fourth sailor missed altogether and plunged down into the sea. I snatched up a boat hook and fished him out before he could be carried away.

For the next few moments the lifeboat bobbed helplessly while I struggled with the boat hook to fend her off from the ship's side. The stern of the blazing *Shantung* was looming over us as she drew slowly past, and there was a horrible risk that we might be sucked into the slowly churning screw. Then Ho Wan got the auxiliary engine running and we had power to pull away. The Bo'sun had the tiller at the stern and mercifully he knew his job without waiting for orders. Our bows turned to starboard and the gap between ourselves and the ship lengthened fast as the *Shantung* got underway.

Once we were clear we could afford to hold the boat steady and relax, taking the opportunity to wipe the soot and sweat away and regain our breath. The salt air was a pure relief in our smoke-clogged lungs and the cool wind a blessing on our scorched limbs and faces. The sea was a long, heavy swell that offered no momentary danger, and the lifeboat pitched and tossed slowly while we who were aboard coughed and sought to ease our hurts and aching muscles.

It was dark now, but the starlight and the flames leaping up from the *Shantung* were lighting up a radius of several hundred yards of the blood-stained seas. The old freighter was a raging inferno, but she still had life, and although she was sinking and listing heavily she was still pushing forward, with her crippled Captain at the wheel and her Chief Engineer still in the engine room. I had not understood why Jean Pierre had bothered to re-start his engines, or why Butcher had ordered me to keep my lifeboat clear from the other two that had escaped, but suddenly I had a terrible premonition of what those two old men of the sea intended.

Ching passed me forward a pair of binoculars and I stood upright again in the bows and searched for the remaining two lifeboats in the black sea. I found one immediately for it was still in the circle of firelight ahead of the *Shantung*. It was grossly overcrowded and there were desperate men still swimming all around it and hanging on to the lifelines, and I guessed that it was the second boat away which somehow they had managed to turn upright again. It was not impossible and desperation can lend dying men the strength of demons.

The first lifeboat, the one that Dinh had launched successfully was further out, perhaps three hundred yards away and still pulling strongly to widen the gap. I ignored it for the moment and turned back for number two. On the bridge of the *Shantung* Butcher had changed the course, and like a blazing funeral pyre of vengeance the old freighter was hunting its prey. The nearest lifeboat was now full in the *Shantung*'s path with the ship looming ponderously over the heads of the screaming men inside. The *Shantung* was making perhaps five knots and bore down upon the helpless lifeboat without mercy. The high steel bows rammed the flimsy wooden craft squarely amidships and buried it and all its shrieking survivors under the black surface of the sea.

It was a ghastly act of retribution for the men who had invaded and soiled, and finally brought about the destruction of his ship, but Butcher had not finished yet. The *Shantung* changed course yet again and steamed slowly but deliberately after the remaining boat with its cargo of Viet Cong.

I realized that pain must have blotted out Butcher's reason. He could no longer think in humane terms but could only act out his final purpose, and his purpose was revenge pure and simple. I knew then that the man I had called Sloppy Butcher had loved his sloppy ship in much the same way that a sloppy man might love a sloppy woman. They needed each other for they were two of a kind. Because he was her Captain he could ill-treat his ship and keep her in disrepair, but he could not forgive these strangers who had taken such blatant liberties with her rusty old hulk.

I had misjudged these two old men, the alcoholic skipper and Jean Pierre, the fading old mimic of Chevalier who was content to die with him. I had faintly despised them but now they were proving themselves magnificent lovers, dying gladly to redeem the honour of their ship. Thang and his Viet Cong had misjudged them too, and now Dinh and those who had survived with him had to pay the fearsome price.

I wondered if Jean Pierre could possibly be still alive in the enclosed hell of his engine room with the great pistons still pounding around him, and decided that if he was conscious he was probably still singing—

"*. . . Thank heaven, for little girls . . .*"

I could practically hear the old Frenchman croaking the words through his raw throat, and I had a brief mental image of Butcher lashed to his wheel on the flame-wreathed bridge with the sweat still running freely down his face.

I had to shake the vision away and focus my glasses again on Dinh's lifeboat. I couldn't tell whether he had the engine running but he had most of his men organized and pulling on the oars. They were bending their backs and glancing behind them with terrified faces, but the fiery torch that was the *Shantung* overhauled them slowly, pitiless and relentless, seeking an eye for an eye, and blood for blood.

Their nemesis was upon them and I saw Dinh at the tiller twisting and turning in a frantic effort to escape. Butcher matched him with every change of course and he would have had more hope of eluding the Devil himself. The bows of the *Shantung* were rearing over Dinh's head when the end came, and the end was abrupt and brutal. Deep inside the old freighter the boilers exploded in a white blast of heat that boomed across the sea like the detonation of an atomic bomb. A pillar of

173

fire soared a hundred feet towards the stars, and the ship was disembowelled and broken in two all in the same stroke. There was nothing but a giant mass of flame and smoke that engulfed the lifeboat, and I could only assume that the bows had ploughed on to carry the smaller craft right down to the bottom. No one could have lived, and what was left of the *Shantung* began to slide below the black waves.

She had been my ship too, and I realized that I had also had some measure of affection for her, and for the two old men who had chosen to accompany her to her grave. I stood to attention and raised my hand to salute their passing. When at last I turned I found that James Ching and Ho Wan were also standing stiffly in the stern of the lifeboat, and they too were paying their last respects. Ching could only salute clumsily with his left hand, and there were tears in his eyes.

The sea became silent and our boat was alone. We were the only survivors.

CHAPTER SEVENTEEN

WE spent two gruelling days in the open boat, a final ordeal under the blistering Asian sun. The nearest land was Vietnam, not more than fifty miles to the north-east, but I set the course south-west for Malaya and with the Bo'sun's help succeeded in hoisting a sail. We had more than forty souls crammed into a lifeboat built to hold eighteen, and most of them had absolutely no desire to return to Vietnam. It was a gamble but we were drifting across the mouth of Gulf of Siam and we were cutting across regular shipping lanes. On the second day there was a puff of smoke on the eye-searing line of the horizon, and I gave Evelyn Ryan the honour of shooting off the flare pistol she had tried to use once before. I loaded it with a smoke cartridge instead of the coloured star shells for night use, and an hour later we were picked up by the *Pascal,* a smart cargo ship registered in Marseilles which was ploughing up from Singapore to Bangkok.

After we had been taken aboard and fed and quartered I spent a couple of hours with the *Pascal*'s Captain, thanking him, telling the long but slightly edited version of my story, and gratefully drinking his whisky. My eyes must have shown the sign of strain, even though I had washed and shaved and generally tried to clean myself up, and finally he packed me off to the bunk that had been provided for me.

I paused on the deck outside his cabin. I had been without sleep for so long that now it had become a weary habit to keep my eyes open. The moment that they did close I would collapse, but in the meantime I crossed to the rail and looked out across the darkened sea. The stars were as bright and glorious as they had been on the night that I had been seduced by Lin Chi, and it was hard to believe that so much had happened and that so much was now hidden beneath the timeless waves. The rail beneath my hands and the deck beneath my feet could have been part of the old *Shantung,* and I had the feeling that it had all been an impossible nightmare, and that if I turned my head the familiar grimy smokestack might still be there.

I had to resist the impulse because there was no escape from reality, and I tried instead to contemplate my future. I knew that soon there would be a vacancy on the *Kiangsi,* the second of our company's microscopic fleet of four tramp ships, and so I need not be on the beach for long. The *Kiangsi* was no more of a ship than the *Shantung* had been, but at least I knew now that even the dirtiest old rust bucket could hold a place in the hearts of the men who sailed her. I had found a belated respect for Captain Leonard K. Butcher, and so I could no longer feel any sense of disillusionment at the prospect of taking over his role.

I was still musing when I heard a movement on the deck below. I looked down and saw the shaven head and yellow robe of Huynh Quoc, and beside him the more bulky figure of Howard Deakin. The old monk had his hands clasped and his head bowed, while Howard stood uncomfortable with his hands on the rail.

"My *Kharma* must be one of black evil." Huynh Quoc spoke with a voice of hopeless remorse. "My past lives must have been filled with terrible deeds, and in this life I have sinned again. All the horrors that we have endured have been my doing, for it was I who helped to conceive the first plan. Every death, and the suffering of every man is upon my conscience."

"You cannot blame yourself," Howard said awkwardly. "Your intentions were basically good."

"I do blame myself! It was my doing! My intentions were wrong!" The old monk wrung his hands and bowed his head more low. "I have learned that a man cannot help the cause of peace by taking up arms or making plans which can in effect only lead to more war.

For what have my plans caused except more death, and pain, and violence?"

"You have saved your friends from Hon San."

"True, I have saved Lin Vien and some others. But count the dead we have left behind us. Most of the men we have saved would rather have died themselves than be saved at such a cost."

"It wasn't all your fault. You couldn't foresee the future!"

"It was my responsibility. Mine was the first sin. I forgot the teaching of Gotama Buddha—a man should seek only his own salvation, and seek it within himself: to become involved in the affairs of others is only to create more suffering and confusion. I have strayed from the Noble Eightfold Path. I have broken my vows! I have shamed my robe!"

His bony hands clutched at his chest and tore at the folds of yellow cloth, and his tone became an agony of hysteria. "I should throw away my robe before I soil it further. I am not fit to wear it. I must go naked to announce my evil heart!"

"Stop that!" Howard pulled the old monk round and gripped him firmly by the shoulders. "Stop it—and listen to me."

Huynh Quoc struggled for a moment, and then became still. He looked up slowly into the round, bespectacled face of the missionary.

"You told me once that there are many paths up the Mountain," Howard reminded him slowly. "If that is so then even if you yourself can slip and fall, the Mountain is still there. The Path is still there! The Path can be regained!"

The old monk was silent for a long moment, and then he nodded.

"You are right. There is nothing that can harm the Mountain or the Path. They are changeless. They are eternal."

"Then go back to your Path." Howard smiled sadly. "I could ask you to come to my Path, perhaps my people would say that I had won a victory to convert a Buddhist priest to the Catholic Church—but I know that

177

it would be wrong. You were right when you said that Jesus Christ showed a light to the west, while Gotama Buddha showed a light to the east. The same compassion spoke through both, and I believe now that they are guides on the same mountain. My soul cries out for the peace of a church, and the sign of the Cross, but yours needs the smile of the Buddha. You must keep your robe. You must go back to the pagoda!"

There was another long silence, and then Huynh Quoc bowed his shaven head in humble resignation.

"You are right," he said again. "There are wise men there who will tell me if I may keep my robe. I must meditate before the Buddha. I must go back to the pagoda."

I had no wish to eavesdrop any further, and so I stepped back quietly from the rail. I walked across the deck to the opposite side of the ship and stood there again to stare out to the stars and the sea. In my mind there was a strange feeling of clarity as I realized that two men had at least learned something from all the senseless death and savagery of the past few days. And I too had learned some things, about other men, and about myself. Perhaps this then was the only purpose of it all? Perhaps in every generation, in every conflict, in every seemingly blind act of war, or stupidity, or violence, a few men learned a little truth each time. And perhaps each lesson was a purge that left the survivors better or wiser men.

While I pondered there was a movement beside me and I turned to find Evelyn Ryan. The Captain of the *Pascal* had his wife sailing with him and the good lady had turned out her wardrobe to find clothes for all our women passengers, and Evelyn was now wearing a skirt and blouse that were at least three sizes too large for her. Her eyes showed exhaustion and her lips were cracked by the sun, but she had borne up well in the lifeboat and now she found me a faint smile.

"Hello, John, are bad dreams keeping you awake too?"

"Not exactly," I said. "There's a lot to think about."

"I know." She leaned on the rail beside me. "While

178

we were in the lifeboat I had plenty of time to talk to Lin Chi's father. He's a very polite and cultured old man. And such a scholar, he told me more than I had ever imagined existed about Vietnamese and Asian art and history. When I began to despair he told me long love poems from the Emperor's court at Hue, translating them into English. I liked him. All he wants for his country is peace. He doesn't want either the Americans or the Communists to win, he just wants both sides to leave the Vietnamese people to find their own future. It's such a simple and hopeless desire that can never happen. You can't disengage two political ideologies at war. One side has to win and the other has to lose."

She looked up at me and came at last to the point that was troubling her.

"He'll be paralysed for life, John. He'll never walk again. What's going to happen to him, and to the others, when we reach Bangkok?"

"They'll apply for political asylum," I said. "I think they'll get it when I make a big enough noise about the atrocities they suffered in the tiger cages on Hon San. At least the Thais will have to let them move on to a country that will give them asylum."

"And what about Lin Chi herself, and the old monk?"

"They were innocent passengers aboard the *Shantung*," I said quietly. "The old monk was forced to lead Thang and his men aboard in fear of his life, but other than that they had no part in it. That's the story I've told the *Pascal*'s Captain, and it's the one I intend to tell anyone else who asks. I know that Hong and Ching and the Bo'sun will all support that story. I haven't approached the Deakins yet but I'm sure of them too. Neither Howard or Janet would ever tell a deliberate lie, but I'll do all the lying and simply ask them to remain silent. They want to do what is right, so their consciences can adjust to that."

I paused and looked at her squarely. "You're the only one I doubt. An agent for the CIA must have loyalties to the faceless men in Saigon and Washington.

You'll have to make out a report for your country. They'll ask you questions."

She looked out to sea for a moment and then said:

"They'll get the same answers that you're giving, and my report will read the same as your story. I know that Huynh Quoc is suffering more inner torment than any human justice could devise, and anyway I don't see how it would help my country just to persecute an old priest and a girl."

I put my hands on her shoulders and turned her towards me, and then kissed her lightly on her freckled nose.

"Thank you, Evelyn," I said.

Her eyes were wide and uncertain, and then she held me and lifted up her face. I kissed her lips and found them rough and harsh, but after two days adrift in the lifeboat my own were in a similar state.

"Perhaps we should have done this before," I said slowly.

"Perhaps."

Her voice was oblique, bending away from certainty, and we both knew that it was too late. She stayed in my arms but her thoughts were flown.

"After I've made my report I'm giving up my job," She said quietly. "I'm not happy with it anymore. This is a grey world, John. Democracy isn't all pure white and Communism isn't all black evil. It's all black and white and grey all mixed up on both sides. When I left the States I believed that the American presence in Vietnam was justified, but now that I've seen all the misery that we have brought to the Vietnamese people I can't believe that anymore. I suppose that in a military and economic sense it is necessary if we are to remain a world power, but there's no moral justification. The Vietnamese are *not* better dead than red!"

She looked up at me and finished: "I took a passage on the *Shantung* to spy on Lin Chi because my CIA Chief told me that her father was a known Communist criminal. I believed a lie and I don't want to believe any more lies. I just want to go home to Oklahoma. I want to watch the wheat grow. I want to listen to the birds singing again."

I recalled my own thoughts about that posssible berth on the *Kiangsi*. There was my only future for I could not leave the sea. Perhaps I could take Ching and Ho Wan with me and we could roam the China seas until we too grew old in our turn. I could accept that now, but still there would be a part of me unfulfilled. I needed a woman to share my life. I looked down at Evelyn Ryan and I knew that she was not for me. There would be no yellow wheat on the *Kiangsi*, and no birds singing. Instead I thought of another woman, a lost soul without a harbour, who already had my heart which had been bestowed unknowingly along with half the stars in the sky.

I said quietly: "Where is Lin Chi?"

"We're sharing a cabin on the deck below. It belongs to the *Pascal's* Third Officer." Evelyn smiled at me, and before she lowered her arms she gave me a brief, parting kiss.

"Good luck, John," she whispered. "I'll give you ten minutes."

I found the Third Officer's cabin and tapped my knuckles lightly upon the door. After a few moments it opened and Lin Chi gazed up at me. She looked little-girl-lost in a large, borrowed nightdress, but her face was the same, smooth classic of Asian beauty. The sun had not burned her too badly. Her black hair was loose and her eyes were tired and perplexed as they met mine.

"Johnny, what is it? What do you want?"

"I want to see you," I said.

I stepped inside the cabin and closed the door behind me, and she looked even more uncertain. I remembered that my butterfly was too fragile to be grasped in a careless fist, and so I kept my hands down at my sides.

"There's something I have to ask you. Perhaps I'm rushing things and it's too soon, but it's in my mind and I have to know now."

She looked blank and I lifted my hands to her arms.

"Lin Chi, I'm asking you to marry me."

Still she seemed to hesitate and I stumbled on:

"I'm clumsy. That was too direct—it's not the Asian way. And I haven't much to offer you, just a shared berth in another ship like the *Shantung*. Maybe not even that. I don't know yet. But something will—"

I stopped because now she was smiling. She came closer and there was a sudden radiance in her eyes. I felt her tremble a little and her voice was an echo from another time as she asked:

"Will you—will you be gentle with me, Johnny?"

"Always," I promised. "As long as you want me to be gentle."

"Then yes, Johnny!"

She came into my arms with a joyous passion, and there was nothing gentle in the eagerness of her kiss.